LJ BURKHART

Of Love and Time

Contents

Chapter 1

Noah— October 5, 2022

"Have a safe flight, man," Damon tells me as I close the door of the R22 helicopter. I've already done all my checks and am ready to take off.

My stomach bottoms out as I ascend into the sky. It's my favorite feeling, and as I get an unobstructed view of the city, I think that this is the life. I want to do this every single day. The city of Portland is spread out before me, and in the distance I can see the ocean. The weather report was clear. I made sure to check before I took off, but you still never know in this part of the country. My flight plan takes me to Astoria, one of my favorite cities.

I didn't always live here. I originally grew up in the Midwest, but I got sick of all the corn that Iowa has to offer, and moved to Oregon a few years ago. I love the Pacific Northwest. I feel like I was always meant to live here. There's ocean, forests, and mountains. What more could someone want? I know a lot of people don't like how cloudy and rainy it can be here, but it's perfect for me. It fits my gloomy personality.

The closer I get to the ocean, the more I can feel my shoulders relax. I love Astoria. I would live here if there was a flight school close by, but it made more sense to go to Portland for that. Whenever I'm able to, I fly here. I like to explore the city and visit all the *Goonies* locations and the shipwrecks close by.

As I start to close in, I notice cumulonimbus clouds ahead. *Fuck.* That's not good. Something must have changed in the hour or so it took me to fly here. I don't see any precipitation, but that doesn't make it any less dangerous. These clouds can produce electrical storms. I consider turning around, but I can see the airport. I think I can outrun the clouds, so I stop admiring the view and kick it into overdrive.

"Astoria traffic helicopter 124AS, altitude 600 on final from the west direct to ramp," I announce my approach.

I'm just getting ready to come in for my landing when lightning strikes. Luckily, it doesn't hit me, but I've had to readjust and regroup. I take a deep breath to calm my racing heart, and in the next second there's another flash and boom right in front of me. I close my eyes on instinct, and it's so bright I'm momentarily blinded.

When I open them again, confusion and fear set in. I don't see the airport anywhere. In fact, *nothing* looks familiar. A cacophony of sounds greets me as my ears stop ringing from the boom of thunder. I think I hear gunshots and see small military planes flying overhead. I look down at my instruments to see them spinning around, not giving me any solid information. It seems as though my helicopter is just as confused as I am about where we are and what has happened. This is not good. A pilot *always* relies on his instruments. *Fuck fuck fuck.*

I hear a plane approaching from behind, and the next thing I know, I feel shots hit the chopper. The helicopter alarms go off, and I curse as I swerve to avoid the next ones. Luckily, I'm already closer to the ground since I was coming in for a landing, because I know this will not be smooth. In fact I might not make it out of this alive. What the fuck *happened*? My heart beats frantically in my chest as I search for a safe space to land as I lose more and more altitude. I find a patch of open land to my right and head in that direction, going as quickly as I can, even though I'm slowing from the shots I took.

Just as I think I'll be able to pull this off and land safely, another round of gunfire comes straight for me. I bank hard, but a shot hits my tail rotor, causing a failure. Everything starts spinning, but I try to maintain my composure enough to land. The helicopter comes down hard, and I lose consciousness.

Chapter 2

Daphne—Vichy, France, October 5, 1940

You'd think after months of this, I'd be used to the sound of gunfire and bombing, but I'm not. I flinch almost every time. At least with the big ones. I try to block it out and focus on the men moaning in pain around me, but fear has my heart beating a tattoo in my chest.

The man currently in front of me is sobbing. He has multiple gunshot wounds. One in his leg, another in his shoulder, and the final one in his belly. I think it's the last one that is causing him so much pain. The first two went straight through his body, but this one is firmly lodged in his gut, and by the way he's writhing on the bed, I would guess it's not anywhere good. One of his organs I would bet. I quickly disinfect and dress the first two before turning my attention to that one. I won't be able to take care of this on my own, so I call for a surgeon. I give him his tools as he works, helping where I can, and holding down the soldier when it's time to pull out the bullet.

When we're finished, I think we might have a moment to breathe, but just as I'm about to sit down and have some water, another man is brought in. My face scrunches up in confusion. He's wearing strange clothing, and doesn't look like a soldier at all. He's unconscious as they carry him over to me. For a moment, I just stare at him. He's the most beautiful man I've ever seen. He has ebony hair, which is shorter on the sides and longer on the top, a strong stubbled jaw, and full lips. I want him to wake up so I can see what color his eyes are. His tanned skin is bloody from the injuries he sustained, and it finally spurs me into action.

"Do you know what happened?" I ask the men who brought him in. The more I know about his injuries, the less I have to guess about his treatment.

"He was in a strange aircraft that seemed to come out of nowhere. He was shot down. When we got to him he was unconscious, and we pulled him out and brought him here."

"A strange aircraft? Are we sure he's ours?"

"He was shot down by the Germans," they insist. "They wouldn't have targeted their own pilot."

"What kind of aircraft was it?"

"A small one. It had blades on the top of it that spun. It moved differently than a plane."

I wonder if there's some secret new invention that's being tested. Hopefully it's ours and not theirs. I thank them and they leave so I can get to work on his injuries. He has a gash on his forehead on the left side, and I'm sure that's why he's unconscious. I cut his shirt open to see bruising along his chest and ribs. I continue cutting along his sleeves to find that his left shoulder is dislocated. I make it to his pants, though the thought of cutting these off makes me blush, but I don't have a choice. I have to make sure he doesn't have any other injuries. I don't find anything else that's concerning, just bruises and scrapes. I tend to his shoulder first since he isn't awake to feel it pop back in. I grab his hand with one of mine, my other supporting the weight of his arm. I take a deep breath, positioning everything correctly before popping it back in. I can hear it the moment it happens, and it spurs the man to finally wake up.

"Motherfucker!" he yells, trying to sit up.

"Soldier, you need to stay down," I order him. "Your aircraft was shot and you were in an accident. I'm tending to your injuries."

"Soldier?" he asks as his bright blue eyes narrow in confusion. It would seem that his concussion is worse than I thought.

Chapter 3

Noah—Who knows when or where the fuck I am

I have no idea why this woman is calling me soldier. I look around the worn tent. It's massive, but looks like it has seen better days. There are dozens of men lying in cots around me. Many of them are moaning or screaming in pain. I hear gunshots in the distance, and it all comes back to me. I was in an electrical storm and then my chopper was shot down. *Shot down.* How in the hell did that happen?

I turn my attention to the stunning woman hovering over me. She's pale with freckles covering her heart-shaped face and petite upturned nose. Her curly red hair sticks out in all directions, but she's made an attempt to tame it with a hairband so it's at least out of her face. Her green eyes look down at me in concern, a pout lines her full, luscious lips.

I blink, making myself focus. "Where am I?" I ask.

"Vichy. The Germans shot your aircraft down."

"The Germans? Vichy?" My heart begins to race as panic sinks even further into my body. I have never been to France in my entire life.

"Yes. The enemy shot you down," she repeats, not understanding why I'm so confused. "You've been unconscious, and you have a concussion. You also had a dislocated shoulder, but I've tended to that already." As she talks, she grabs a length of cloth, bringing it over and wrapping it around my neck and under my elbow, creating a sling for my arm. I move around to help her secure it. It's a little awkward with me lying down, but she manages. "You also have gash on your head that I need to stitch up, and then you need to rest." I realize then that while she claims we're in France, her accent is English.

I try to take that all in, but am in too much shock to do anything besides lie there. How is it possible that I traveled to another country? And why was I shot down by Germans? I don't keep up with world events most of the time, but as far as I know, Germany and France haven't had any problems with each other for a long time. In fact, the last time I can think of is World War II. I suck in a sharp breath. *No. It's not possible.* I look at my surroundings again. I do not feel like I'm in my own time. Based on the clothing people are wearing, I would guess I'm in the forties.

The nurse comes back with a needle and I know she's about to stitch up my face. Do I dare ask her what I think is happening? I mean, now would be the best time since she's assuming I have a concussion. Well, I *do* have one, but I don't think that's the reason for my confusion. Fuck it. "Miss…?"

"Daphne." She provides me with her name as she wipes at the gash on my forehead with alcohol, disinfecting it. I wince slightly at the sting.

"What's the date?" There. That's a safe enough question.

"October 5," she replies.

Fuck. It was October 5 when I took my flight. Still… "What year?"

She stills, the needle halfway to my face. "Year?"

"Yes."

"Nineteen forty."

I can feel all the blood drain from my face, and I fear I'm going to pass out again.

"Hey. Take some deep breaths in through your nose. Breathe with me."

I do as she says. It's difficult at first, but after a minute or so, I'm able to keep it going and the lightheadedness passes slightly. It makes so much sense now. Well, as much as time travel *can* make sense, if that is what indeed is going on. The reason I was shot down. I'm in France in 1940. I was shot down by the German army.

"What type of aircraft were you in?" Daphne asks, probably to distract me as she gently shoves the needle through my face. "I heard it was an unusual one. The men who pulled you out of it weren't sure what it was."

Fuck. How do I even answer this? I might as well go with the truth. She won't have heard of it anyway. At least I don't think she would. I can't remember when the first practical helicopter was invented. "It's called a helicopter."

Her brows furrow in confusion. "I don't know what that is. Is it a new invention? Is our military creating new weapons against the Germans?"

"You could say that," I say. I think it was invented in either the late '30s or early '40s. "When you say the Germans…" I trail off, not knowing how to ask this without sounding crazy. I guess it won't sound any crazier than asking her what year it is.

"Yes?"

"Are they Hitler's army?"

Her lips purse, and I can't quite discern the expression. "Of course."

Fuck. It's official. I've somehow traveled to Vichy in the middle of World War II. I'm so fucked.

Chapter 4

Daphne

I stare at the man in front of me. Why is he so confused? I know he has a concussion, but it doesn't make sense for him to be *this* disoriented. I finish his stitches, which he takes better than most men. What can I say? Men are babies. I know he's going to have a scar, and I dare say it will make him even more attractive.

"Do you need some water?" I ask. He looks a little pale and lightheaded.

He nods absentmindedly at me, seeming stuck in his own thoughts. I understand. I can imagine that getting shot out of the sky by some pissed-off Germans would be disorienting. I grab him a glass of water, set up some pillows behind him as he sits up to drink, and urge him back against them when he's finished.

"Do you need anything else right now? I need to tend to the

others." I'm half hoping he'll say he does so that I have an excuse to stay, but with the sounds of distress and pain around me, I know that's an incredibly selfish thought.

He shakes his head, and I leave him to tend to another soldier who was just brought in. I work throughout the day, but am constantly aware of him. I don't know what it is, but there's something about him that's different and interesting. I can't put my finger on it. He's handsome, but almost in a way that doesn't fit.

I try to ignore him, but it's like magnets are constantly pulling my eyes to him. He hasn't moved much since I left him there. He seems lost in his thoughts, and if I didn't know any better, I would say it seems like his whole world was just turned upside down.

I finish my rounds and finally come back to him. "How are you feeling…?" I realize then that I don't know his name.

"Noah."

"Nice to meet you, Noah."

"Nice to meet you too, Daphne. And I'm fine. A little sore, but nothing compared to most of these men." Sadness touches his tone as he looks around in respect and admiration.

"Just because you didn't get as injured as they did doesn't make what you do any less noble," I tell him honestly. I'm floored daily by how brave these men are. They protect us and those who can't protect themselves.

"I'm not noble or brave," he says dejectedly. I'm about to contradict him when he finally looks at me. "Thank you for your help today. And just so you know, you're just as brave as all of these men here. Most of them would be dead without what you all are doing."

I feel uncomfortable at his compliment but tell him thank

you anyway. "Is there anything else you need before I leave?"

"You're leaving?" His mouth turns down in displeasure.

"Yes, but I'll be back first thing in the morning. There will be a night nurse here, though, if you need anything."

"I won't. I just enjoy watching you work."

I blush. Not the other nurses. *Me.* I don't quite know how to respond, but I wonder if he feels the same pull toward me as I do to him. "Well, I will be back tomorrow. But you should be well enough by then that you can return home or to your base."

I immediately know I've said the wrong thing when his eyes shutter and disappointment colors his features. "Yes, I suppose so. Well, I'll see you tomorrow then."

I smile at him before getting him another glass of water and leaving. As I walk out and head to my home, my heart beats faster at the thought of seeing him tomorrow.

Chapter 5

Noah

uck me. I've been trying to wrap my head around my predicament all day. How did this even happen? Was it the electrical storm? That's the only thing I can think of. How am I going to get back home? Am I stuck here now? Amid all of that, my brain continually circles back to the redhead. Daphne. She's beautiful. Like classically beautiful. I've never seen anyone else like her in fact, and I wonder if it's partly because I'm in a different time period. And then I come back around to the fact that I somehow time traveled.

I'm clearly a mess. It's too bad she had to leave. She was the only thing keeping me from focusing on the present and not feeling completely insane. I have no idea what I'm going to do when they essentially kick me out tomorrow. I'm pretty sure the only reason I still have a cot is because of my nasty concussion.

Maybe if I find a way to get back to my helicopter I can learn something. Although, I have no idea where it's even located. For all I know, the Germans destroyed it. Not like I could fly it even if I wanted to. I'm sure it's wrecked beyond repair just from the bullets and the crash.

The next nurse to show up is much older and much crankier than Daphne. She reads over my chart before shining a bright light in my eyes. I cringe away from it, as it sends shooting pain through my skull.

"You need rest. Go to sleep," she orders. "I'll be waking you throughout the night."

I groan at that, although with everything that's happened, I'm not sure if I'll be able to sleep. I close my eyes anyway, figuring that I can at least try to lessen my pounding headache. Before I know it, I'm drifting off into a restless sleep. My anxious thoughts from the day follow me into my dreams, and I experience the crash more than once. The sound of explosions and gunfire continues to echo through my head, and I can't tell if it's real, or if it's only in my dreams.

The cranky nurse continues to wake me every few hours, and even though I know she's just doing her job, all I want to do is sleep and escape from this reality. Although, my dreams aren't much of an escape at this point.

After a few hours of restless dozing, dawn lights the horizon, and I give up on sleep. Excitement builds in my stomach as I think of seeing Daphne again. I don't know why I'm so drawn to her. Is it some sort of Nightingale effect? I noticed how much her gaze strayed to me yesterday. I would've flirted with her a bit if my head hadn't been so fucked up, not to mention that she was literally saving the lives of dying soldiers. And she thought I was one of them. Fuck.

As if summoned by my thoughts, Daphne breezes in, looking just as beautiful as she did yesterday. Her eyes immediately find mine, and I give her a dashing smile. She blushes and returns it. She sets her things down and goes to wash up. She checks in with the night nurse and tends to the patients that need it the most, but I've noticed that today isn't very noisy. Hopefully the Germans have moved onto a different spot.

After about an hour or so of her seeing to other men, she finally comes to check on me. "Good morning, Noah. How are you feeling?"

"Better now that you're here. Nurse Scowl woke me up all night."

She chuckles. "You mean Nurse Nancy? Yeah, she's not the friendliest, but she's wonderful at her job."

"If you say so."

She checks over my shoulder, removes the bandage on my forehead, cleans the stitches, and rebandages it. When all that's done, she looks into my eyes with a light like Nurse Nancy did last night, but this time it's not as piercing.

"Overall, you look pretty good. You should be able to leave us today."

I nod, my dread and anxiety returning. I don't know what to do now. I never figured out a plan. "Okay."

She helps me sit up, and I soak in her warm, calming touch. Her eyes shoot down to where our hands are clasped together, and I wonder if she likes my touch as much as I like hers. Just as I'm about to ask her about it, or comment, or *something*, I hear a loud boom and multiple screams.

"They've infiltrated the city! They're coming for the camp!" someone shouts from right outside our tent.

All hell breaks loose, and within seconds, German soldiers are pouring into the space. Luckily, my cot is at the edge of the tent. I act without thinking, clutching Daphne's hand harder and pulling her with me under the flap of the tent, and somehow we escape.

Chapter 6

Daphne

On the other side of the tent, Noah looks into my eyes. "We need to be as quiet and sneaky as we can. If they're really in the city, we'll need to find a place to lay low. At least for the next day or so. Understand?"

I nod, my heart racing and palms sweating. I always knew this was a possibility, but I was hoping that I would never have to be *in* the action itself. Looks like that hope has been lost. It takes all of my willpower to follow Noah as we slink around corners and not stop to help those I hear screaming. But deep down I know I can't do anything for them right now, and that if I were to attempt it, I wouldn't be able to help anyone later on.

We move along through the city, and I think we're just about in the clear when I hear a group sweeping the area. Noah hears it, too, and pulls me into the closest alleyway. He presses his body in close to mine, hiding us against the wall of the building. My heart beats even faster as his proximity and scent stirs up something neglected in my body, and I fight to stay in the present.

"Check the alleyway on the right!" someone shouts close by, and my breathing comes faster in panic. Luckily, Noah keeps his head and pulls us farther into the shadows.

"Look, there's a door here." He tries the handle, and I don't know what we did to get on God's good side today, but it's miraculously unlocked. We sneak inside and Noah locks it behind us. We stay up against the door, listening for the scout. I jump a foot in the air when the handle is jiggled from the other side, but somehow manage not to make a sound. I hear them yell "All clear!" and my heart rate finally starts to slow down.

We relax against the door, and it's then that I notice we're still holding hands. I can feel myself blush as I finally pull away from him.

"Where are we?" Noah whispers.

I look around. It's a large building, but there doesn't seem to be much actually *in* it. "I think we're in one of the closed-down factories." When the war started, a lot of the factories that were making things designated for "peacetimes" were either shut down or converted to make something that was necessary for battle.

He nods as he looks around. We make our way farther into the building. Upstairs we find what was once a break room. An old couch is still there as well as a rickety table with a few chairs. One wall is full of windows, and we carefully peek out down below to see what's happening.

There's soldiers sweeping through the city slowly but surely. Those who they find are bound, bagged, and taken. I watch closely for where they're leading them. If there's any shot of freeing them, I want to take it. I take note of each location, and notice a few are actually close by in other closed warehouses.

"Noah, I know it's too risky right now, but I think we should try to find a way to free them."

"Daphne, I don't think that's a good idea. There's just the two of us and the only weapon we have is my little pocket knife."

"Okay. You're right. But let's at least keep track of where they are in case we come up with some kind of plan."

He nods before resting his back against the wall. "Fuck me. What have I gotten myself into?"

I wonder if he joined the military willingly. It sounds like he did, and is now regretting that decision.

I take stock of him and notice that his brace for his shoulder has shifted after all the running around we did. I lean over and gently readjust it. I then check the bandage on his forehead, which looks fine, before checking his eyes. Those look clear too. The most clear they've looked since I met him. I get lost in them, and for a moment we just stare into each other's eyes. It's an incredibly intimate moment, and when I realize it, I break away, looking around us instead.

"I wonder if there's anything else here," I muse aloud.

"I'll go check it out. I need to make sure all the entrances are locked."

"Oh, I'll come with you."

"No. You should stay here just in case. There's no need for you to endanger yourself further. Stay put and I'll be back soon."

Chapter 7

Noah

I walk away from Daphne and mentally slap myself. What the fuck am I doing? I can't get involved with her. Yes, she's beautiful, yes, she's kind and sensitive, and yes, so far she checks every box. Oh, except for the fact that she lives in a different *time period* than me. Jesus. Get it together, Noah.

I make my way downstairs and go into every room I can find. A rat or two scurries out under random debris multiple times, startling the shit out of me. I'm not typically jumpy, but being on high alert with the German army on our ass is not a normal situation for me.

I check the doors, and they're all locked up tight. I have no idea why or how that specific door was left open, but I'm thanking the universe with all I have in me for the save. I do *not* want to be in a POW camp right now. Or ever, for that matter.

When the first floor is clear, I head back upstairs, mentally preparing myself for spending so much time in close quarters with Daphne. I almost leaned in to kiss her when she was staring into my eyes earlier. Luckily, she broke the spell and I didn't make things even more complicated for myself. I need to get back home. But even if I knew how, I wouldn't be willing to leave with her stranded here on her own.

Once we get to safety I should try to find my helicopter. I still don't know if it was something to do with the aircraft itself, or the electrical storm I was caught in, maybe a mix of both, but if I can examine it, maybe I can learn something. I'm grasping at straws and I know it, but at this point, I can't think of how else to get home.

I methodically check all the doors and windows in the factory, and am grateful that they're all secure. There's not much here, but I come across an old blanket. It doesn't smell great, but at least it will keep us warm. The warehouse is drafty, and it's fall in France. I'm more than a little chilled.

I slowly make my way back to Daphne. I try not to think about her too much, but I can't help it. If my mind isn't on the whole time travel thing, it's on her. I can't get attached to someone in a different time period. What happens when I go home?

I'm also assuming that she would even be interested. Maybe I'm just being a typical guy and thinking that she wants me, when in reality she's just stuck with me because of our situation.

On my way back to her, I come across a set of bathrooms. Luckily, there's still running water, and I wonder how long this place has been shut down. I use the restroom and take a drink from the faucet. We don't have food, but at least we have the most important thing. Who knows how long we'll be holed up here. I can't imagine it would be safe to go wandering around the streets anytime soon.

Daphne is right where I left her, still staring out the windows as if willing the POWs to spontaneously break free.

"Everything's clear. All the doors and windows are locked. I also found this blanket." I set it down on the couch.

"Thank you," she says, not taking her eyes off the buildings. "I suppose we'll need to stay here for a while."

"I think that's smart. And who knows? After watching where they have all the hostages for a day or two, maybe we can come up with some way to help them after all." I can't help but give her some hope. It looks like that is the only thing she's thinking about.

Her gaze whips to mine, and a small smile graces her beautiful face. "What do you want to do in the meantime?" she asks.

"I think the only thing we can really do is talk and get to know each other."

She smiles even more fully at that. "Well, soldier, what do you want to know?"

What do I want to know about her? The answer to that is simple, but not one I can give her. *Everything.*

Chapter 8

Daphne

I look at the handsome man in front of me and wait for him to ask me a question. I can't help but stare at him. There's something about him that's so alluring, and just *different*. I still can't put my finger on what it is. And I almost swooned when he mentioned the hostages. I don't know if we'll be able to manage it at all, but at least he's willing to try to come up with something.

"What made you want to become a nurse?" he finally asks.

"Nothing in particular, I've just always enjoyed helping people and looking after those in need."

A softness enters his eyes, and I blush under his scrutiny. "I think that's a very wonderful and selfless trait to have."

I wave him off, uncomfortable with the compliment. "What about you? How long have you been a pilot?"

"A few years now."

"Have you been with the military that whole time?"

He clears his throat uncomfortably. "No."

He doesn't elaborate, and I wonder why he's acting so strange. Before I can ask him, he's on to his next question.

"You're not from here are you?"

"No. I'm originally from Surrey. I moved to France a few years ago. When the war started, I joined the army as a nurse. I already had some training, but it's different out here as opposed to a hospital, so they had to teach me a bit more. And you're from America?"

"Yes. I grew up in Iowa but I've been living in Oregon for the last few years."

"You don't live in the UK?"

His eyes widen slightly, and he blinks slowly at me. "No."

"What are you doing here then?"

"Honestly, Daphne, I have no fucking clue."

I chuckle. "I understand. It's hard to remember why I decided to do this when I'm faced with the reality of it day after day."

"That's not… I mean, yeah, that makes sense. Is your family still in Surrey?"

I narrow my eyes as I wonder what he was going to say originally, but decide to let it go. "Just my mother. My father died ten years ago of tuberculosis, and my brother is fighting in the war. I don't know where he's at right now. His troop moves around a lot."

"I'm sorry. That must be hard."

"It is what it is. My mother did a damn fine job of raising us after he passed, and I helped when I could since I'm the oldest. I got a job as soon as I could to pitch in with the bills. And it can be scary having my brother on the front lines, but he really wanted to take down some Nazi bastards. I know he's being as safe as he can be right now. Do you have any siblings?"

"I do. I have six sisters, all older."

My brows jump in surprise, and I chuckle. "Wow. That must've been hard growing up."

"Eh. It was basically like I had seven mothers. Except the ones closer in age to me liked giving me shit once in a while. I'm grateful though. I think because of that, I've come to have a much deeper respect for women than most men have. I saw everything they went through, and I realized very young how strong women are."

A smile graces my lips, and I reach over to squeeze his hand, taking him by surprise by the look on his face. "I think that's wonderful. Thank you for seeing our strength. You're right, most men don't appreciate it or recognize it."

He gives me a shy smile, and I swoon a little when a hint of a blush comes to his cheeks. I wouldn't have guessed he'd be bashful.

"What's your favorite color?" he asks, turning the conversation to something less serious.

"Purple, of course. Everyone knows it's the best color."

He laughs boisterously. "I would have to disagree with you, my lady. Green is clearly superior."

"Then why do royals wear purple and not green?" I inquire.

"Because they're pretentious," he states matter-of-factly.

I smirk. "Well, I can't argue with that."

We get more comfortable on the couch, settling in for who knows how long.

Chapter 9

The next few hours are spent asking any and every question we can think of to get to know each other. Despite the fact that we're from different time periods, I'm surprised to find we have a lot in common. We both have laid-back personalities and a similar sense of humor.

The longer we talk, the more comfortable we get with each other. The attraction begins building even higher between us, and I scoot closer to her on the couch. I have the urge to pull her feet into my lap and rub them for her, but we're not there yet, and I don't want to make her uncomfortable. I also grew up in a very touchy-feely family, so I try to keep in mind that a lot of people aren't as comfortable with touching as I am.

My breath is taken away when she smiles wide and laughs at the jokes I tell her, making me want to tell them again and again. Her smile absolutely lights up her face, and I can't look away.

"Are you romantically involved with anyone?" I ask her. I'm not sure how people talk in this time, but I don't know if she would understand what I mean if I asked if she had a boyfriend.

A blush rises to her beautiful cheeks, but she smiles shyly at me. "No. Are you?"

"Not in the slightest," I reply as I give her a flirty smirk.

We start getting hungry and thirsty. I leave her on the couch to look around the "kitchen" in the break room. I find a glass that's a bit dirty, but will work nonetheless. I rinse it out a few times before filling it with water and bringing it to Daphne. She drinks greedily, and before I can stop myself, I'm staring at her throat working, inappropriate thoughts starting to swirl there. When a little path of water slides from the corner of her mouth down her chin, I have to turn away to keep myself from leaning in to lick it off.

I search all the cabinets and come across a can of tomatoes and a jar of peanuts. I bring them over to Daphne and grab the glass to refill it for myself. I chug the whole thing before refilling it again and returning to the couch. She has the peanuts open but not the tomatoes since I didn't give her anything to open them with. I search around the kitchen for a can opener, but can't find one. Luckily, I always have a pocket knife. It won't be the prettiest thing, but I should be able to get it open enough to get tomatoes out.

After a few minutes of finagling with it, I jaggedly remove the lid, whooping in my triumph. Daphne claps next to me, and I soak up the praise, feeling like I just accomplished something much bigger than opening a can of fucking tomatoes. We dig into our measly meal, but I'm grateful for it all the same. It takes the edge off our hunger, and allows us to stay here for a little longer, lost in our own bubble. When we're finished, we sink back against the cushions.

"You can sleep if you want. I can keep an eye out."

At my words she yawns. It's only the afternoon, but she was up early, and it's been a scary and eventful day.

"Are you sure? I could use a nap, but it isn't necessary."

"Get some rest. We'll need it for whatever comes next. We need to be at our best. I'll watch over you." I trail my fingers along her cheek, finally giving in to the urge to touch her.

She gives me a shy smile. "Okay. Thank you, Noah."

"You're welcome, Daphne."

She settles into the couch and rests her feet in my lap. My heart squeezes at the contact. I'm so fucked. "Whatever happens, I'm glad I met you."

She drifts off within minutes and I'm soaring at the fact that she trusts me enough to be this vulnerable with me. While she sleeps, hopefully either undisturbed or with pleasant dreams, I try to plot and figure out how we can get the hostages out of custody without drawing attention to ourselves.

Chapter 10

⚜

Daphne

I wake several hours later, judging by the position of the sun in the sky. Noah is in the exact same spot. My feet are still in his lap, and a slight blush comes to my cheeks at the intimacy of it. He locks eyes with me and a smile graces his lips, his hands squeezing my feet affectionately.

"Mornin', sunshine."

"It isn't morning," I respond, rolling my eyes.

"How do you know?"

My heart beats a little faster, and I wonder if it really is morning. Then I realize that he's just teasing me, and I narrow my eyes at him in mock anger. I kick at his chest half-heartedly, and he laughs before catching my foot and tickling me. I squeal and thrash. I'm deathly ticklish on my feet, and I really do end up kicking him with how hard I'm struggling. Whatever. He deserves it. That is, until I accidentally kick him in his bad shoulder and he hisses in pain.

"Fuck, I'm so sorry. Are you okay?" I scramble up to check on him.

"I'm fine, I just forgot about this damn thing."

I reach out and touch his shoulder, not trusting his judgment. It does in fact feel fine, and I breathe a sigh of relief.

I hit his good arm. "Don't do that! We have enough to worry about without you injuring yourself further over something stupid."

"Aw, are you *worried* about me?"

I roll my eyes. "Only because I don't want to have to patch you back up."

He clutches his chest in mock pain. "*Ouch.* You sure are vicious when you want to be."

"Something to remember." I stick my tongue out at him.

He laughs, but his eyes zero in on my lips, which are now wet with my saliva, and his hands clench.

I blush and pull my feet out of his lap finally, steering us away from the intimate moment I could feel creeping up on us.

"Anything happen while I was sleeping?"

"No," he sighs, a regretful look on his face. "I've just seen soldiers come and go from where they have the captives. It's hard to tell how many are keeping watch, but I think there's at least one inside with them. We would have to get closer, though, to really be able to tell."

"Do you think we should try?"

"I think we should watch them for a while longer. Try to figure out a schedule and see when they switch guards. The last switch was about two hours ago."

My brows fly up in surprise. "I've been asleep that long?"

He nods. "You were tired. Your body needed the rest."

"I know you're right. I haven't been sleeping much with the war going on. I've been working more than I'm used to."

I stand and get more water, feeling parched after my long nap. I take another peek through the kitchen, hoping there's something we didn't see earlier. When I find nothing, I wonder what we should do next. I mean, we can't stay here forever waiting for the Germans to slip up so we can rescue everyone. Or if by some chance we get lucky and that does happen soon, we can't return here.

"Do you think we should try to make a run for it to my home? We'll need food sooner or later." I don't want to be stuck here anymore, but I'm not sure it's a good idea for us to leave yet.

He gazes at me for a brief moment before turning to look out the window again. "I don't think we should yet. I'm sure they're still out there trying to round up more people. And we have no idea what state your home is in. It could be even more dangerous there. At least here we're relatively safe as long as we don't give ourselves away. Maybe in a day or so we can try."

I nod, thinking along the same lines. I'm grateful I have him with me. It would be difficult to make these kinds of decisions on my own. I've never been a woman to rely on others, but I have to admit that it feels nice.

Chapter 11

Noah

We spend the evening getting to know each other more, but as the day wears on, my exhaustion peaks. I slept horribly the night before, and my body is trying to recover from the crash, not to mention the threat of being caught by the Nazis. As my eyelids droop for the hundredth time, Daphne finally says something.

"Lie down."

"No, I'm fine. I don't want to hog the couch," I insist.

"You don't have to be a gentleman. Your body needs to recover, which means you need good rest. I'm plenty comfortable sitting here. You can put your feet in my lap like I did with you earlier. We'll both be warm that way too."

Before I can object again, she pushes me down and covers me with the blanket we found. It doesn't smell great, but I'm not about to complain. She pulls my feet into her lap, and my heart pounds faster. We've obviously gotten more comfortable with each other throughout the day, but this feels different to me. I don't think I've ever been like this with a woman who wasn't my family before. It's comforting and exhilarating.

Despite my objections, I'm asleep within minutes. I'm grateful that Daphne lets me sleep and doesn't wake me incessantly like Nurse Scowl did last night. My dreams are plagued by nightmares again, so it isn't restful, but it is deep. Still, something wakes me hours later.

I open my eyes to see that the sun has set, and Daphne is passed out at the edge of the couch, her head resting against the back. Chills erupt over my skin, and the back of my neck prickles. Something is wrong. I'm sure of it. I slowly glance around, my eyes straining in the darkness. I palm my pocket knife, freeing it from my pants and sliding the blade open. I can't hear or see anything, but I can't shake the ominous feeling.

I stay alert, even after minutes, and finally I see something. Or should I say, *someone.* A dingy-looking man is creeping around the factory. His gaze zeroes in on Daphne, and his eyes light with malicious intent. Anger burns in my throat, almost spurring me to act, but I hold steady. I need to wait for him to come closer so I have a better chance of stopping him. He somehow still hasn't noticed me, and I pray that my luck holds.

He slowly creeps forward, and when his hands start reaching for Daphne, I lunge. I jump over the back of the couch and tackle him to the floor. I think Daphne wakes with a shout, but I'm so absorbed in the man that I don't pay it any mind. We scuffle for a few minutes, moving farther from the couch and Daphne. We each get some good shots in and are in the kitchen before I remember my knife. I hold it up to his neck.

"Stop right now, motherfucker. I will not hesitate," I growl.

He stops struggling and raises his palms in surrender. My hands are shaking with the rage that's built inside me from what I suspect he was going to do to Daphne. A snarl rips free from my throat as I think about him laying his hands on what's *mine.* There's no time to give that possessive word any thought, but I'm sure it'll pop up later.

Daphne walks up to us slowly, as if approaching a wild animal, which I can't deny I feel like right now. When she's close enough, she lays a gentle hand on my arm.

"It's okay, Noah. You stopped him in time. Nothing happened," she reassures me. I don't know how she can tell that I'm about to go against my word and lose my shit, but her words turn my vision less red and hazy.

I don't take my eyes off of him, but I take some deep breaths in through my nose and out my mouth. That helps even more. When I feel somewhat more composed, I think of our most immediate concern.

"How did you get in here? All the doors were locked."

He swallows against the knife. "I picked the lock. I needed someplace to hide from the Germans, and I thought there might be some food in here." I can barely understand him through his thick accent.

"How did you pick it?"

"I stole a lock-picking set a few years ago. It's done me good on the streets."

I look down, eyeing his pants. We could sure use that. I had a friend who was interested in lock-picking a few years ago, and we fucked around with his set for a while. I was never great at it, but maybe with some practice I could use it on the hostages.

I'm trying to figure out how I can convince him to give me the set, or wondering if it would be smarter for me to just take the thing since I already have my knife to his throat. I look at Daphne, ready to tell her to search his pockets, when I feel him shift against me. I tense just as she yells, "Noah, look out!"

Chapter 12

Daphne

The man underneath Noah surges up, grasping Noah's knife hand. They scuffle back and forth, fighting for dominance. Luckily, Noah is stronger than Crazy Man, but obviously Crazy Man is more, well, crazy. It's difficult to predict his movements, and suddenly, he reaches up to start choking Noah. I rush forward to help before he loses consciousness or drops the knife.

I grasp his nasty hair tightly and throw his head back against the concrete floor to knock him out. At the same moment, Noah slashes the knife forward, nicking him in the neck. Blood spurts out, soaking us both, and Noah jumps back in startled surprise.

"I didn't mean to do that!" he shouts, panicking.

"I know," I say calmly as I straddle the guy and apply pressure. Unfortunately, it looks like Noah got his carotid, and there's really no coming back from that. "Noah, can you rip a section of my dress off the bottom?"

He does as I ask, even though I can feel his hands shaking. He hands it to me, and I wrap it around the man's neck as tightly as I can without cutting off his air supply before applying pressure again.

"He was going to hurt you," Noah says quietly behind me, and I know he's trying to justify what he had to do.

"I know. It's okay, Noah. You protected me. You also warned him not to move, and he did anyway. He would've killed you just as quickly if given the opportunity. I'll do everything I can to save his life since I'm a nurse, but if he does indeed end up dying, don't blame yourself for it."

He doesn't say anything else, but I can feel him pacing behind me. There's nothing I can really do except to keep pressure on the wound, especially since I don't have anything to stitch him up with. Within minutes, the man's heart beat fades against my palm and I pull back in resignation.

"He's dead." Before I stand, I wipe my bloody palms off on his shirt and rifle through his pockets. He said he had lock-picking tools. We could use those. I don't know the first thing about it, but maybe Noah does. And we could always practice on the doors here.

It takes me a few moments, but I finally locate the two small metal pieces. I realize then that Noah is starting to hyperventilate behind me. My brows furrow in confusion and concern. Death isn't ever easy or fun, but with our current situation, I figured he would have become acclimated like I have. War means death. Unfortunately that's the way it is. And with him being a soldier, he has to have witnessed it countless times by now. I know I have.

"Noah?" I ask hesitantly.

He doesn't seem to hear me. He's pacing and frantically running his hands through his hair, making it stick up on end. He's muttering under his breath to himself, and I strain my ears to catch the words.

"No no no no no no no."

He's having a panic attack, I realize. I slowly get up and walk toward him like I'm approaching a cornered animal. I make sure to make noise so I don't startle him, and when I get close enough, I set my hands gently on his shoulders, stopping his forward progression. His eyes snap to mine, and they're frantic.

"Noah, I need you to sit down for me." I lead him over to the couch and nudge him so he obliges. I kneel down in front of him so we are eye level. "Good, now put your head in between your knees."

He once again follows my orders, more quickly this time. "Now, listen to my breathing and copy it. In and out slowly." I exaggerate my breaths, and after a few minutes, his shaking subsides, and he seems to be calming down.

He lifts his head finally and looks at me. A dozen emotions I can't name swirl in his eyes, none of them good. "Thank you."

"What happened? What caused your panic attack?"

"I've never killed someone before. I know that he would've done the same to me, and was *trying* to. Not to mention that he tried attacking you while you were sleeping. But still, I didn't *want* to kill him."

My face scrunches up. That doesn't make sense. "How can you not have killed someone before? You're a soldier in this bloody, violent war."

He takes a deep breath and thoroughly searches my eyes, looking for an answer to a question I don't know. "Daphne. I'm not a soldier. I'm not a part of this war. I'm not even from this *time.*"

Chapter 13

Noah

Fuck. I can't believe I told her that. My mind is so fucked up from what just happened. And I couldn't lie to her. She knew it wasn't normal for me to react that way. Not for a seasoned soldier. I can tell by the look in her eyes that she either thinks she misheard me or that I'm crazy.

"Excuse me, what?" Her voice is hard; maybe I was wrong and she thinks I'm trying to fuck with her.

I sigh heavily. I shouldn't have said anything. I don't feel up for telling her what happened, especially with her reaction. "I don't belong here. I'm from the year 2022. I know that sounds impossible, and it *should* be. I have no idea how or why it happened. I was in my helicopter in America coming in for a landing when I was caught in an electrical storm. The next thing I know, I'm being shot at and my helicopter crashes."

Skepticism lines her eyes, but I take it as a win when she

doesn't immediately tell me off and call me a liar. "So, do you know how this war ends?"

I nod. "Not all of the details. History was never my favorite subject, but I know it ends in 1945. Hitler commits suicide and then the Nazis surrender, and Japan surrenders later that year after America drops two atomic bombs on Hiroshima and Nagasaki." I'm glad I at least know that much.

Her eyes widen as that information sinks in. I don't know if she believes me or not, but if I wasn't telling the truth, it would be damn hard to just pull that lie out of my ass.

"It's going to last another *five years*?" Tears build in her eyes, but she doesn't let any of them fall.

I nod sadly and sympathetically. "I know it's terrible. It's the worst war in our history. Where I'm from we haven't had a World War III yet, and it hopefully stays that way."

Her eyes narrow in suspicion again. "How do I know you're telling me the truth?"

I sigh. "I'm not sure, Daphne. Honestly, I don't even know *how* this happened. If I did, maybe that would convince you. We could try to find my helicopter. I think that would do it. It will be more technologically advanced than *anything* you've ever seen. I need to find it anyway. Try to see why I came here in the first place."

She nods like I've pacified her concerns, and I wonder how I managed to convince her that I'm telling the truth. Or maybe she doesn't believe me yet, and is waiting until we can go investigate my aircraft.

"What you're telling me is insane, but a small part of me isn't surprised. From the second I saw you, I knew you were different. Especially when you woke up. There's something about you that doesn't fit in here, and now it makes sense. You're from a different *time*. Jesus."

I laugh despite myself. "You know, you have a much dirtier mouth than I would've thought for a woman in this time period."

She chuckles and rolls her eyes at me. "I'm a war nurse, Noah. I'm around soldiers and trauma doctors all the time. It wears off on us."

"I've always liked a woman who curses as much as I do," I tease, smiling as a blush rises to her cheeks. It's a relief to have a bit of levity to even out the seriousness of the situation.

When reality sets back in, we look down at the man I unintentionally killed. Panic rises in my chest again, making my heart beat faster, but it's thankfully not as intense as before. I remind myself that he was going to harm Daphne. He was trying to kill me. It doesn't make it okay, but it helps me to settle a little bit.

"What should we do with him?" I ask.

Her brows furrow in thought. "Maybe for now let's just find an empty room far from us and put him in there. We won't be here for too much longer, hopefully."

I walk back over to him, but before I can pick him up, Daphne is at my side, her hand going to my back. "It wasn't your fault. Thank you for protecting me," she says softly, laying a gentle kiss on my cheek.

Despite our surroundings, heat rises within me, and before I can stop myself, I'm leaning down to capture her lips with mine.

Chapter 14

Daphne

Noah's mouth meets mine with a desperation I feel in my soul. It's like we've known each other for years instead of days in that moment. Something about him awakens something inside of me that I can't name.

My lips part as his tongue slides against them, giving him access. He takes full advantage and he plunders inside. It's a claim. One I am all too happy to allow. I wrap my arms around his neck, pulling him closer to me. It seems to snap something inside of him, and he groans low in his throat as he grips me by the waist and hauls me against his body even more fully. We're plastered together, and I can feel every hard ridge of his muscles pressing against me.

My hands develop a mind of their own as they wander over every bit of his body I can touch, and I'm delighted when he makes a low noise that almost sounds like a purr. His teeth nip my bottom lip, and a whimper escapes me as my nails dig into his shoulders. I'm suddenly *desperate* for him.

I push him to where I know the couch is, and we clumsily make our way there. I plan to shove him onto it, but before I can, he's gently lowering me down without even breaking the contact of our mouths. I moan in delight when I feel his weight cover me, and I think the only thing that could make this better is if we didn't have clothes on. I start pulling at his shirt, desperate to feel his skin against mine.

He breaks away to accommodate me, and between the two of us, we have it off in seconds. My gaze sweeps over his torso, taking him in in all of his glory. He's *magnificent*. My fingers lightly graze over his chest, and he closes his eyes as he hums. I can feel the vibrations in my hands, and I smile at the sensation. I love that I can affect him this way.

When he opens his eyes, they're blazing. His own hands wander to my own clothing, and I take no time in helping him to remove them. Whatever has sparked between us, there's no stopping it now, not even if I wanted to. When my body is bared to him, he drags his gaze slowly down every inch of naked flesh.

"Stunning."

I blush under his praise as it heats every bit of my soul. Before I can say anything, his mouth is dragging a line down my neck to my clavicle and then my breasts. Everywhere I feel his touch, goosebumps are left in his wake. When his lips close around one of my pert nipples, I gasp as the sensation travels directly to my core. I whimper and grasp his hair, holding him tight to me. When he nips at my skin, I almost shoot off of the couch. I can feel his smile against my skin, and I tug on his hair in retaliation. He laughs in earnest then and brings his mouth back up to mine.

I run my hands along his toned chest, delighting in the shivers that rack his body. For a little bit of payback, I dig my nails in slightly, giving him just the barest hint of pain with his pleasure, and it's my turn to smile when he growls against my mouth. He breaks away from my mouth and trails his lips to my ear. He's breathing just as heavily as I am, but whispers in my ear.

"I've wanted you from the moment I saw you. You're unearthly in your beauty. You consume all in your path, and I'm done resisting you."

I melt against him as his words register. I've never had anyone speak to me like that before. I love it.

"Then take me," I tell him, as if it's as simple as that. As if his words don't rock me to my core.

His heated eyes meet mine, and it's as though he's staring for an answer written into my soul. Whatever he finds there, it seems to give him what he's looking for, and he dives back in to claim my mouth in a fevered kiss.

Chapter 15

Noah

Daphne's mouth tastes like heaven. Like honey-covered heaven. Her hands are fumbling with my jeans, and even though I know I should take it slow and make sure she's okay with this, I don't have the willpower. Especially when she clutches my hard cock through the denim. I growl into her mouth, my control snapping.

I break away from her, needing the space to focus on getting the rest of our clothes off. Her mouth is a drug, and while addicting, I'm not able to think straight when I'm getting high off of her.

She whines when I pull away, but it turns into a gasp as I yank her panties down her legs. When she's fully naked, I drag my gaze over every inch of her.

"I could stare at you all day."

"Please don't. I need you. And it's your turn to take your

pants off. I want to see you too," she all but orders me, and I harden even more at her tone.

I give her a cocky smile as I slowly unbutton my pants and slide them and my boxers down my legs. She sucks in a sharp breath as she surveys me, and I puff out my chest unconsciously at the ego boost.

Before she can do or say anything, I drop to my knees in front of her. I spread her legs wide, groaning at the sight of the wetness seeping from her.

"Noah, I—"

I dive in before any more words leave her beautiful mouth. If I thought her mouth tasted sweet, it's nothing compared to her pussy. Within moments, she's writhing under me, gripping my hair with both hands. It's almost as if she's trying to pull me closer and push me away at the same time. I grab her hands and pin them to her sides, torturing her with my tongue. She moans her pleasure out, and I delight in the fact that I can do this to her.

I suck her clit into my mouth, flicking it rapidly. I want to keep her pinned in place to have my way with her, but I want to use my hands on her even more. I release her hands and they immediately resume their position. This time, however, she doesn't push me away at all. She holds me close and starts bucking her hips wildly against my face.

My left hand goes for her nipple, twisting and tweaking, while my right hand drags up her thigh, only one destination in mind. I spear a finger into her, delighting in the way her wet heat clenches me greedily. She starts getting louder, and as much as I love it, we're in too precarious of a situation for that.

"Daphne, you need to be quiet. We cannot be caught. When we're out of this, I want you to scream my name to the heavens, but if you don't shut that pretty little mouth of yours, I'm going to have to stop. You don't want that now, do you?"

"No, please don't stop. I'll be quiet. I promise."

I grin. "I love when you beg me."

"Noah," she warns, desperation lacing her voice.

"What do you want?" I know, of course, but I want her to tell me.

"Your mouth. Make me come. Please. I'm going crazy."

Because she asked so nicely, I dive back in without another word. I can't get enough of her taste, and I feast on her. She brings my shirt back up to her mouth, holding it there to muffle the noises she's making.

"Good girl," I praise.

I plunge a second finger into her and she shoves her hips down to impale herself further. *Fuck.* This woman is going to be the death of me. I'm so hard it hurts, and I palm myself to relieve some of the ache that's built there.

Her movements become more frantic above me and I double my efforts. "Come for me, Daphne. Come against my face." My voice is a low rumble against her flesh, and she shivers.

Her hand pulls frantically at my hair in her mindless pleasure, and when I suck hard on her clit, scraping my teeth lightly there, she explodes on my tongue, her inner walls squeezing my fingers continuously. Her other hand is holding my shirt tight to her mouth, dampening the sounds of pleasure pouring from her lips.

I slowly continue to lick her, gently bringing her down from her orgasm. When she goes limp under me, I pull back slightly, kissing her thigh tenderly.

She lifts her head and gives me a sated smile. I sit up and bring my lips to hers. I devour her mouth, letting her taste herself, and when her breathing speeds back up, she pulls away. "I need you." Those words break what little self-control I had.

Chapter 16

Daphne

I'm delighted when I see Noah's eyes flare with heat in the darkness at my words. He rises above me, coming to lie on the couch with me. I sigh in pleasure as his weight settles over me. His cock brushes against my opening, and I whimper with need. I want him inside me so badly.

I shift my hips against his, coating him in my wetness, and he groans into my mouth. "Daphne. *Fuck.*"

"What do you want?" I echo his words back to him. My turn to make him beg.

His eyes narrow, a knowing look there. "That's not fair."

"Oh, it's not?" I ask innocently. "Well, we can just stop, if you want?"

He growls at me before slamming his lips against mine once more. I chuckle against his mouth before breaking away.

"What do you want, Noah?" I want to hear him tell me, just

like he did.

"I want to feel your cunt milking my cock." He gives me exactly what I want with those words, and I close my eyes at the deliciousness of them.

I reach down and grip his hard length, reveling in the way he pulses against my palm and groans deep in his throat. I stroke him a few times before bringing him back to my opening.

"Fuck me, Noah."

He indulges my request and plunges inside me with one thrust. I gasp, not expecting it to feel as heavenly as it does. I clutch his back in desperation as he starts to move. Every time he withdraws from my body, my walls clench, trying to keep him there. It's exquisite and I never want it to stop.

My nails score his back with every movement, and I fight to keep the sounds contained in my body. It's so difficult to remember that we have to be quiet, but Noah seems to understand as he brings his mouth to mine again, swallowing any noises that break free from my lips.

His hand trails down my body and stops at the bundle of nerves there. I'm still sensitive from my orgasm, and I shudder and sob against his lips. He swirls his thumb mercilessly against me and I feel myself building again.

I break away from his kiss. "Noah, please," I beg. I don't exactly know what for, but he seems to.

He pulls out of me and flips me onto my stomach. I don't even have time to protest before he's filling me again. His fingers dive between my legs once more, keeping up their tortuous rhythm, and his breath fans out on my neck. He sucks my earlobe into his hot mouth as his fingers pinch my clit, and that does me in. I detonate around him, screaming my release into the couch. He slows his thrusts, and I notice he hasn't found his release yet.

"Noah?"

"Hmm?"

"You haven't come yet?"

"Oh no. I'm going to give you another orgasm before that can happen." He says it so confidently that I huff in surprise.

"I don't know if I can again," I whimper.

"Of course you can. And next time when you squeeze my cock like that, I'm going to fill you so full."

Another burst of desire hits between my legs unbidden. I've never had a sexual experience like this before. I don't know what to do with myself. He tweaks my nipple, causing another shoot of pleasure, and I sob. I am torn between wanting him to keep going and stop. I'm so sensitive that it hurts so good.

He changes the angle of his hips just the slightest, getting deeper than before and increasing his pace, and the decision is taken from me. The pain dissipates, and pure pleasure surges through me. I shift my hips, grinding against his relentless fingers and his cock, chasing another orgasm.

"That's it, love. You take me so good. Are you going to come for me again?"

I whimper and moan, nodding my head. I'm beyond words right now.

"Good. I'm so close, but I need to feel you strangling my dick again."

His words send me over the edge, and I plummet off of it, soaring to all new heights. I thought the last two were intense, but they were nothing like this one.

"Fuck. Oh *fuck*, Daphne," Noah groans in my ear, and then he's coming and twitching inside of me.

I don't know how long we lie there catching our breath, but

when our heart rates and breathing begin to slow, Noah slides out of me. I move as far over on the couch as I can manage to make room for him, and he lies next to me, bringing his arm around me and holding me close.

I close my eyes as I sigh against him, completely satisfied.

Chapter 17

Noah

I hold Daphne tight in my arms as we drift off. Despite the fact that we're on an old, worn-out, small-as-fuck couch, I sleep better than I have in my entire life. When I wake, though, I'm reminded of the fact that I killed a man last night. Ice slides through my veins, but it's not the pure panic I experienced after it happened. I'm sure part of the reason is the woman in my arms.

I revel in the feel of her warm body pressed tight against me. I told her the truth last night. She didn't freak out. And I think she believes me. That brings another set of issues though. Now that I've had her, I don't think I can leave her. I don't *want* to leave her. At the same time, I also don't want to be in this time period. I don't want to experience years of war. I know that this isn't an easy time to live in.

I also have no idea how to even get back to my time, or if it's possible. So at this point, I guess it's pointless to worry about it.

Daphne stirs, mewling softly like a little kitten, and it has to be the cutest thing I've ever heard.

"Good morning, gorgeous. I wish I could offer to make you breakfast or coffee, but under the circumstances all I can do is get you a glass of water. Thirsty?"

She chuckles against my chest. "Not yet. I'm enjoying this too much."

I smile and tug her closer. I'm enjoying it too. "We'll have to get up soon. There are things we have to do today." I regret bringing it up when she tenses.

"Yeah, I know. Do you have a plan?"

"I think so. At least a general one. This morning I would like to practice with that lock-picking set. Once I master that we can make a plan for sneaking over to free the hostages. From what it looked like, I think there are only maybe two guards inside. I'm pretty sure the other ones take shifts outside. If we can sneak in between two shifts then we shouldn't have to get around a ton of them. The part I'm getting hung up on is *where* we're going to take them when we escape."

"Well, most of them live here in the city. I'm sure if we just give them a chance to escape, they'll all be able to sneak back to their own homes."

My eyebrows rise. I feel stupid for not thinking it was that simple. "You make a good point."

"Women do sometimes have good ideas," she remarks sarcastically.

I tickle her instead of responding because I can't think of a good comeback. She giggles and wiggles against me.

"Noah!" she squeals, and I chuckle, finally relenting.

When the moment is over I sigh. "As much as I would like to

stay like this all day, we should probably get up."

She nods, standing. I admire her naked body in all its glory. The sunlight silhouettes her, making her look like an angel, and I have the desire to drop to my knees and worship her.

"If you continue to look at me like that, we'll never get anything done."

I grunt, but rip my eyes off of her. She's right, but I promise myself that when we are out of this mess and safe in her home we will have a proper night together. One where she can be as loud as she wants and we will have an actual bed. I get hard thinking of all the things I'll be able to do to her with enough room, but shake my head to clear the inappropriate thoughts.

I stand and dress, and when I turn I see the dead body lying in the kitchen. Bile rises in my throat, but I swallow it. I have a job to do, and it's time to get to work.

I grab the blanket, knowing we won't be here long enough to need it again. I wrap his body in it, cringing at the amount of blood that's left behind. I sling his body over my shoulder and head off to the farthest point in the warehouse.

I dump his body in one of the empty rooms. This one is windowless and I hope it will at least help with the smell. I feel bad leaving his body here for someone else to find, but we don't really have a choice.

I shut the door and head back to the break room. It's time to get practicing with that lock-picking set.

Chapter 18

Daphne

Noah spends all day practicing with the lock picks. In turn, I camp out in front of the window on the floor to watch the guards, trying to discern when they switch shifts. The first one was this morning at seven, according to Noah's watch. It's fancier than any watch I've ever seen, and I guess there's some of the proof that I was looking for.

It takes a few hours, but when they switch again, I run off to find him. He's not too far off, having found a lock to practice on nearby. He looks up as I approach.

"What time is it? They just switched."

He looks down at his fancy watch. "Eleven. So we can assume that they switch every four hours."

"So, the question is whether or not we want to attempt it at three or seven. What do you think?"

"I think it would be smart to get more practice in with this before we attempt it. Then we can also confirm that it's four hours. We'll have the cover of darkness to help us out too."

I nod, thinking along the same lines. "How's the practice coming along?"

"Pretty good, actually. These locks are easier than the ones from my time, but they're slightly different, so it took me a minute to get the feel for it, but it's going much smoother."

"How long is it taking you now?"

"I'm down to about three minutes on average, but I think I can cut that down in the next few hours."

I nod, impressed. I just hope it's short enough for us not to get caught sneaking in. I did see a discreet entrance that's off from the main doors that I think we'll be able to use. It doesn't look like they walk by it too frequently, and earlier when they switched it took a few minutes for the new guards to show up.

"Do you need anything?" I ask him.

His stomach chooses that moment to growl loudly. He sighs dramatically. "I wish we had food, but I guess I'll settle for some water."

I rub his back in sympathy. I am just as hungry, and the thought of having to wait for at least another eight hours to eat makes me want to cry, but I don't think about that. We have people to save.

I head off to the kitchen, mindful to avoid the massive bloodstain taking up the front section of the floor, and fill our water glass. I drink a decent amount myself before refilling it and bringing it to Noah. The liquid helps to make me feel just the slightest bit less hungry. Hey, I'll take what I can get.

I hand it to him, watching him gulp it down. Inappropriate thoughts rise as I think of what he was able to do with that mouth of his last night. Heat blooms in my core, and I chastise myself. We don't have time for this. To distract myself, I try to remember the food I have at home, fantasizing about what we can eat when we get there. It's an equally bad idea, and brings my hunger back full force.

"Did you see any of the other buildings they were taken to? Or just the one closest to us?" Noah asks, snapping me out of my thoughts.

"I saw the general direction, but not the actual buildings. Did you?"

"No. Honestly, I'm a little relieved about that. I don't know if we can do this more than once, and I think we would both feel obligated to try if we knew where the other hostages were."

I nod. "I think one will be enough for now. There's only two of us after all."

"And we can always tell someone who would be better equipped to handle this after we're safe. We know the general area they're in."

A knot loosens in my chest. I like that idea. And I feel better about having a plan to help the others. If we survive, that is.

"Okay, well, I'll let you get back to it. I'm going to keep watch at the window just in case. Let me know if you need anything."

I lean down to give him a quick kiss, but it, of course, turns heated before I can pull away. We're both breathless when we finally break contact.

"I could get used to that." He smiles sweetly at me, but his words bring a touch of dread to my mind. Will we get the opportunity to be an actual couple? Between the mission we were embarking upon, and the fact that he doesn't belong in this time, I have no idea what the future has in store for us.

Chapter 19

Noah

Hours later, Daphne confirms that the shift change happens right when we predicted it. I take an hour or two to rest. My hands have been cramping for a while, but we'll have only one shot at this and I don't want to fuck it up.

Daphne brings me more water and massages my hands. After the work they've done all day, I groan at the contact. She hits all the right spots, and I realize that's because she works with her hands day in and day out.

I keep an eye on the clock, and time seems to drag and fly by all at the same time. On one hand, I'm very excited to get out of this shithole with a dead body in it. I'm starving, and I want to take Daphne to *bed*. Not to a couch. On the other hand, I'm terrified it's all going to go wrong and I'm somehow going to get us killed or captured.

Ten minutes before it's time for them to switch, we sneak out of the building, making our way around the back where we came in. I peek my head around the corner, checking to make sure the coast is clear. When I don't see anyone, we run quickly but quietly across the street. I'm thankful for the cover of darkness, but the problem with that is that *we* can't see as well either.

We duck into a space near where we're planning on entering and I get to work on the locks. I know it's going to take me a few minutes to get in, and I should have it done by the time the first round of guards leave. Usually there's a minute or two between when the first guards leave and the next show up. I'm praying to whatever Gods are listening that that's the case now.

Daphne keeps watch behind me, and I can hear when the first set of them tromps off, exhausted. I don't have it in me to feel relief. I have no idea when the next set is showing up.

All the practice I did earlier pays off, and I'm opening the door to the building just under two minutes after I've started. I don't know what we'll find on the other side, and I slowly edge it open. I almost startle when I find a guard on the other side, but am relieved when I see he's dozing off. Our luck seems to be holding. I sneak up behind him and work my arm around his neck. I'm not going to kill anyone if I don't have to, and this way I can just knock him out.

When my skin makes contact with him, he stiffens. I clamp my hand around his mouth before he can make a sound and squeeze tight with my arm. It takes forever, and my muscles are burning with the strain by the time he finally slumps in my arms. I let out the tiniest sigh of relief as I set him down as quietly as possible. I wish we had rope or a gag or something.

Daphne seems to have the same thought. "Rip off another

section of my dress," she whispers. "We can use it to tie his hands. It's better than nothing."

I do as she says, and there's just enough material to bind his hands behind his back. I tear off a section of my own shirt as well and stuff it in his mouth before tying another section over his lips and behind his head as a gag. Not bad.

Daphne hands over my knife, having held it just in case we were caught while I was picking the lock. I grasp it, feeling marginally better having it in my palm. Daphne tries to go ahead of me, but I don't let her. I'm not going to let my woman head off into dangerous territory before me. I guide her to stand behind me and we start making our way through the building. We have no idea where the hostages are being held, or what we'll find here, but we have to try.

Chapter 20

Daphne

We made it into the building. I can't believe we were even able to accomplish that. My heart is beating out of my chest as we sneak around inside. I'm sure that one of the guards is going to hear it and catch us. I'm pleasantly surprised at how steady and calm Noah seems to be. I shouldn't be considering how well he did when we escaped, but the fact that he's not from this time and not a trained soldier makes it even more impressive.

We wander for what feels forever, and I start to worry that we have the wrong building. But just as I'm about to ask him if we should try to come up with a different plan, we hear voices. They're speaking German so we can't understand them, but there are only two. We hunker down around the corner, waiting to see what they'll do. Their voices rise, and I wonder what they're arguing about.

Suddenly, we hear footsteps approaching and I realize they've stopped talking and one of them must be walking away. Right toward us. Noah backs us into the empty room down the hall and quietly closes the door. We hold our breath until his steps fade.

"Okay, I think it's just the one guard left. Hopefully the hostages are with him or close by and we can leave," he whispers directly in my ear.

I nod and we ease the door open. I let Noah head out first since he would protest otherwise. I smile at the thought of him being so protective, but admonish myself. This isn't the time to be swooning.

We head back to where the men were arguing and Noah peeks his head around the corner. He turns back to me and nods quietly before slinking off. I follow him and am finally able to take in the scene before me. There's a fairly large open space and the other guard is facing a door. He's shaking his head and muttering to himself. It's then that I see his gun, and my blood turns to ice. This *can't* go wrong. Why did we choose to do this? This is so incredibly stupid. Noah sneaks up behind him, sticking to our plan instead of running for the hills.

When he's directly behind the guard, he carefully reaches out and snags the gun. Unfortunately, halfway through the act, the man pulls on the weapon, and instead of it ending up in Noah's hands, it flies across the floor. The two men are scuffling now, but Noah learned quickly from our incident last night. He pulls the knife on the Nazi soldier, but the man disarms him before he can do anything with it, and it drops to the ground. My heart sinks with dread. This is *not* how this was all supposed to go. I rush over just as Noah tackles him to the ground. They're matching each other blow for blow until the man gets Noah onto his back, his hands around his neck.

Noah punches him in the ribs and anywhere he can reach, but the man isn't letting go. I have to do something. I snatch the knife off the ground, and thank my lucky stars the man hasn't seen me yet. I know I won't be able to get the best of him if I try to spare his life, and if I don't do this, Noah will die. All because this was *my* idea. Resolve hardens my heart and I step up behind him and insert the knife in the man's temple. He slumps forward, dead before he realizes what even happened. Relief floods me as color starts returning to Noah's face.

Noah stands in front of me, gratitude shining in his eyes. "Thank you for saving me." He leans in and gives me a soft kiss, expressing everything he's feeling without needing to say anything else.

When he pulls back, I bend down to grab the knife out of the German's skull. It's disturbingly difficult to remove, and if it weren't for the fact that I've seen some disgusting things as a nurse, I would be shuddering in revulsion. I hand it to Noah before grabbing the gun off the ground. We will use it only as a last resort, but I feel better now that we have another weapon.

Noah kneels in front of the door after confirming it's locked and starts picking it. It takes him even less time, and then the door is open. I gasp in relieved shock. We found the hostages.

Chapter 21

Noah

I gape at what I see before me. There are about thirty people packed into this room. It smells awful already, even though they haven't been here long. They rush toward us as we open the door, and I realize too late that they don't know we're here to rescue them.

Daphne reacts before I do. "It's okay! We're here to save you!" She raises her hands in a gesture of peace.

They keep running toward us, and we quickly back out of the room. I realize their plan was to rush whoever unlocked the door as soon as it opened. They just thought it would be their enemy, not people trying to save them.

They are too far gone to listen to reason, so I pull Daphne with me, heading back the way we came. Just as we're about to round the corner and disappear toward the exit, we hear their footfalls stop, and one yells out to us.

"Wait! You're really here to help us?"

I wonder what got them to stop, but when I turn around, I see that they've noticed the dead guard.

"Yes. We saw them bring you all in here. We were hiding out across the street and came up with a plan to sneak in here. We can show you where we came in, and with luck, we can get back out unnoticed. You all can go home. We have to be quiet though. There aren't many guards, but I would rather them not know we were even here."

The leader of the group, a middle-aged man, studies me intently before looking down at the dead man again. He meets my eyes, nodding and gesturing for the others to follow.

We're quiet as we make our way through the empty hallways. I have no idea where the other guard went, but we have our weapons at the ready and our eyes peeled for any sign of movement.

We reach the door we came in with the still-unconscious guard, but just as we are about to enter, the other guard comes in from a separate door. He swears under his breath and approaches quickly, examining his comrade. We have seconds. I know he will notify the others, and our cover will be blown.

He swings around just as I rush forward. He cries out in alarm, but luckily not loud enough to alert anyone. We collide in a storm of fists. I know he has a gun, but we're too close to each other for him to get a good shot.

I have a brief moment where I can't believe that this is something I'm actually living. I've had three deadly altercations within the last twenty-four hours. That isn't me. I haven't been in a fight since middle school.

Unlike the last two instances where it was just me and Daphne, I have a whole group of people to help me. I'm not fighting him long when two men drag him off me, holding his arms out so he's immobile.

Before I can warn them, he starts yelling. I shoot forward and clamp my hand over his mouth. He bites me and I curse, but keep my palm there. I can't risk the others coming.

Another one of the hostages grabs his gun and hits his head with the butt of it, effectively knocking him unconscious. I breathe a sigh of relief as I reclaim my hand. It's bleeding, and I curse the fucker. He bit me hard.

"I can wrap it for you," Daphne whispers to me.

I shake my head. "Not right now. No time. We need to go before anyone else comes to investigate."

At that, I crack the door open and peek my head out. I can't see anyone. I close the door again and turn to the group, speaking quietly but loud enough that everyone can hear me.

"The guards are to the right. We don't know what things look like to the left, but I think that will be our best bet. It will be smartest if everyone splits up and goes their separate ways. We will be much less easy to spot if we aren't in a huge group."

Everyone nods, and the leader comes up to me, shaking my hand. "Thank you. Both of you."

We nod and I clasp his shoulder. This is it. We did it.

Chapter 22

Daphne

The hostages all insist we go first for a few reasons. We have a better idea of what's going on outside and can help guide everyone. They also want to make sure we don't get caught after helping them. The sentiment touches my heart, and I have a hard time not making sure they all get out safely, but they're insistent.

Noah pops his head out again, checking that the coast is still clear. When he doesn't hear or see anyone, he waves us forward. A small group of us sneak ahead, and I lead the way. Noah doesn't know where to go.

I grab his hand so we don't get separated. He hangs on tight, and I wind us through the streets of Vichy. The group behind us dissipates as we continue to trek forward. They all go toward their own homes and lives.

My home is a little farther away, but I'm grateful for that. I'm really hoping that my area of town will have been left alone.

When we finally reach my street, I sigh in relief when I see things looking completely normal here. No doors have been knocked down, and I even see a few of my neighbors lingering on the street.

"We're here. We made it."

Noah squeezes my hand tightly, as if he doesn't believe it. I don't believe it myself. We rescued a group of hostages without the guards being any the wiser. I just hope everyone made it home safely.

I lead us up to my door, unlocking it. I pull him inside, and I finally let myself relax when the familiar scents of home flood me.

"Shower or food first?" I ask.

"Food then shower. Then I want to take you to bed and worship you all night."

His words make my core clench and my toes curl. I like the sound of that.

I head toward the kitchen and open my fridge. My stomach growls angrily, now that I know I'm finally able to eat, and I debate on what to start with. Since we're in the middle of a war, I'm usually pretty careful about how much I eat, but I'm too hungry for that right now.

I pull out hard cheeses, wine, veggies, cottage cheese, and bread. I'm too hungry to actually make anything until I get some food in my stomach. Noah opens the wine as I start cutting slices of bread and cheese for us. We each eat multiple servings, and I moan as I wash it down with wine.

"Fuck me. I was so hungry. I didn't even realize until now," Noah comments, making me laugh and nod.

I take some bites of cottage cheese, and when my stomach

doesn't feel quite so empty, I chop some veggies. Noah jumps in and helps, and between the two of us, we have a nice selection ready to go.

I get a pan and some oil ready on the stove and throw all the veggies on before heading back to my bread and cheese. I'm still eating quickly, but I can't help myself. I occasionally stir the pan, and by the time the veggies are done, I'm not quite so ravenous. Noah and I basically demolish the rest of the food, and I chuckle at how quickly it disappears.

I plate up the food, refill our wine, and we bring everything to my dining table. It's strange to think that I had shared my body with this man before we'd broken bread together. Literally.

We eat not quite as quickly this time, but we're still much too involved with our food for talking. When we finish, Noah is about to grab the dishes, but I grasp his hand and pull him with me to my bedroom. I want to get clean with him. And dirty.

Once we enter the bathroom I turn the shower to near scalding before stripping off my soiled clothes and throwing them in the trash. Noah follows suit, and we're in the stall moments later. I moan enthusiastically as the hot water trails over my body. This feels heavenly after what we just endured.

My body finally relaxes, and I delight in the sensation. I'm so focused on the feeling that I start when Noah's hands glide down my wet body. I open heavy-lidded eyes to see that his are on fire as he admires me. He gathers the soap in his palms, and in the next second he's washing me.

I've never had someone pamper me like this before. Usually I'm the one to take care of others, and I have to admit, it's wonderful.

"You're spoiling me," I remark.

"You deserve to be spoiled. I'll give you everything you want if it's in my capability to do so."

Tears pool in my eyes at his words. "All I want is you."

"You have me. Always."

That calms the fear that he's going to head back to his time without me, and I'll never see him again. I don't know when I started fully believing his story, but I don't doubt one word of it.

But if we somehow find out *how* he traveled here, and find a way for him to return, the question now has become do I want to go with him, or should we stay here?

Chapter 23

Noah

When we're thoroughly clean, and have fooled around only a *little* bit, I scoop Daphne in my arms and carry her out of the shower. I set her down and dry her off before taking care of myself.

She's so selfless, always giving parts of herself to those she takes care of. It's an honor to be able to do the same for her. I can tell no one ever has before, and the thought makes me sad. I promise myself then and there to remember this. To always take care of her and see to her needs.

I pick her back up and settle her gently on the bed. I can already see wetness dripping from her and my mouth waters. Before I can act on the urge to devour her, though, she sits up on the edge of the bed. My eyebrows quirk in question, but I let her continue. She runs her hands down my thighs, and then her lips wrap around my pulsing length.

I groan in surprise and delight. Her mouth is heavenly. My fingers twine in her wet hair as I hold it out of the way for her, but I let her control the movements. I wasn't expecting this from her in the first place, but I'm blown away when she takes me all the way into her mouth. Her eyes leak a few tears as I pulse against the back of her throat.

She bobs her head up and down on me, her eyes never leaving mine. The heat in them could send me over the edge alone if I let it. But I don't want to spill myself inside her mouth. Not this time.

I grip her hair a little harder and pull her off of me. She releases me with a wet *pop.* Before she has a moment to recover, I'm attacking her mouth with mine.

"You drive me crazy, woman."

Her legs spread beneath me. "I need you. Noah, please."

Without another word, I thrust into her. We moan in unison when I'm fully seated inside her. Her wet heat envelops me, and I have to fight with myself not to lose control right then and there.

I take a few moments to compose myself, kissing her senseless instead. It doesn't keep her occupied for long though. Her heels dig into my ass urgently.

"Noah. *Move.*"

I do as she commands, pulling out before pushing forward as slowly as I can. I want to make this last, even though I'm sure it will be a hopeless endeavor. I'm able to maintain the pace for only a few thrusts before she's flipping me in a move I was not expecting.

I'm lying back and suddenly she's riding me with the force of a hurricane. It's so sexy that she's taking what she wants and needs from me. Even if I wanted to give it to her slowly, there's something to be said about her taking control.

"Fuck. Daphne, I don't know if I can last much longer."

I need to move her along. I take advantage of my position and feel along the length of her body, tweaking her nipples and stroking her clit with my thumb.

"Oh, please," she begs, upping the tempo even more. I can tell she's close with every squeeze of her cunt around my cock.

I catch her off guard and sit up, bringing our chests tight together. Her lips crash to mine in a desperate kiss, and I fuck her mouth with my tongue just as thoroughly as I dive between her legs. With one more stroke of her clit, she's detonating around me. She's milking me so hard that I'm thrown headfirst into my orgasm, calling out her name.

We sit there catching our breath, our chests rising and falling against each other's, and when our heart rates have finally settled, we collapse onto the mattress beneath us.

I tuck her into my side, more content than I've ever been in my life. As we drift off, I know she's meant for me. Whatever happens, we need to stay together.

Chapter 24

Daphne

Noah and I sleep for twelve straight hours. It feels so nice to not have to worry about being attacked or caught by the Germans. While we technically slept in the warehouse, it wasn't restful. We were both on edge, especially after the intrusion. I shudder as I think of all the things that could've gone wrong.

When I wake, I'm curled around Noah. We collapsed in exhaustion as soon as we finished making love, a combination of the adrenaline rush from rescuing the hostages, overwhelming pleasure, finally being able to eat, and just regular old not sleeping well the night prior, ensuring that we were asleep as soon as our heads hit the pillow.

I stretch like a cat in the sun after a long nap. I'm pretty sure a mewl escapes me too. The noise wakes Noah, and he growls low in his throat as he pulls me tight to him. As much as I love this, I have needs I have to take care of. Not to mention that my mouth feels like something died in it.

I extricate myself from him, much to his dismay, but he'll end up thanking me later. I take care of my body's needs before brushing my teeth for longer than I have in a while. When I'm finished, Noah switches spots with me. I consider taking another shower, but decide against it. I try to conserve water and cut down on any bills. We are in the middle of a war after all.

"Hungry?" I inquire.

"Starving."

I chuckle at that. We had enough to eat last night to feed double the number of people, but I guess since we hadn't eaten in a while our bodies burned through the food fairly quickly.

"I'll make us some breakfast. Meet me in the kitchen when you're done here."

I head into the kitchen and check my fridge. I take out the eggs, bread, and Spam. I cook the meat in its own pan, cutting a round hole in the bread before buttering both sides and putting in the other pan and cracking an egg in the hole I left. I add one more for me, and while that's cooking, I find some oatmeal in my pantry.

I know I've been going overboard with meals since we got to my apartment, but we deserve to indulge after all we went through and accomplished.

Noah comes out soon after and lays a heated kiss on my lips. I delight in the minty freshness of it. I hum against his mouth in pleasure, wanting to stay like this forever.

He pulls back before I burn anything. "Coffee?"

I nod, pointing to the cupboard above the machine.

He sets to work getting it going, although it seems a little clumsy and confusing for him, but he figures it out without any help. I wonder briefly how they make coffee in the future. That thought brings a slew of curiosity with it. I want to know all about the time he lives in. I try to picture myself there with him, but I have no idea what things are like, so it's impossible. But I *want* to picture it.

If I was able to, would I want to travel back with him? The thought is scary, but also exhilarating. Not to mention that I wouldn't be in the midst of the deadliest war this world has ever known. I would miss my family, but as it is, I rarely ever see them.

I'm overthinking this. I don't even know if Noah will be able to return. Or if he *wants* to return. Or if he'd even want me to come with him. I've known him only a few days after all. Wow. Is that all? It seems like so much longer.

"I can see the wheels turning in your head over there. What are you thinking so hard about, baby girl?"

His question snaps me out of my spiraling thoughts. "Oh, nothing."

"I'm calling bullshit," he replies lightly, hip-checking me.

I return his hip-check, and he's knocked off balance by my wider hips.

I sigh. "I'm just thinking about what happens now."

"How do you mean?"

I decide to tell him something that I've also been thinking about that's slightly less complicated. "I'm wondering who we should tell about the other hostages. And obviously our camp was invaded. I don't know where I should go to report for my shifts."

He looks at me as if he can tell I'm not telling him everything, but he lets me off the hook. "Well, I'm assuming you have a headquarters you can report to?"

I nod. I can kill two birds with one stone that way.

"Want to do that today?"

"Yes. I want to make sure they have the best chance possible at saving those hostages. And the longer we wait, the higher the possibility that they'll relocate."

He nods in understanding. "I'm also wanting to see if we can find my helicopter, too, at some point. I don't know how safe it will be in that area though."

My heart pounds harder at the thought of what we'll find. Will I end up losing him before I've truly had him? Dread seeps into me, but I force a smile. "We can see. They typically move on fairly quickly from an area."

Chapter 25

Noah

Daphne and I eat breakfast, just enjoying each other's presence, but even though we're safe at the moment, clean, and well-fed, I can't help the anxiety that builds with every passing moment. I feel like there's a metaphorical ax that's hanging over our heads, reading to drop at any second.

Luckily, Daphne has some of her brother's clothes here from when he's stayed with her in the past. I'm so grateful that I don't have to put on my filthy, bloodstained outfit that I've worn since I arrived. I'm a little bigger than him, so they're a tad tight, but I make do. Better than the alternative.

When we're ready, we give each other a look before we leave. It seems we're both uneasy about this and reluctant to part from this sanctuary, even though we know it's necessary.

I bring her in for an embrace. I tell myself it's not a goodbye, but I have a feeling that's a lie. I kiss her with all I have in me.

I'm not ready to say the words that I shouldn't be feeling yet, but she seems to understand all the same, her hold tightening on me.

When we pull apart, our breaths are uneven, and I think I see tears in her eyes before she blinks them away.

"Ready?" she asks, false cheer in her voice.

I nod, not having the strength to do the same.

She locks the apartment, and we hop in her car.

My brows rise in surprise. "How is your car here? Didn't you take it into work?"

She shakes her head. "I typically bike to work. Much less expensive, and it doesn't take me too long. But we're going too far to walk right now."

She drives us across the city, and it's so strange to see how different things are. I didn't really have the opportunity to think about it before this, but now that I'm able to see daily life, it's more apparent than ever. Life just moves at a different pace than I'm used to, and the city has more than been touched by war. Those I see are evidently exhausted and thin. Much thinner than people in my time.

I'm so distracted by the world I'm completely unfamiliar with passing us by that when the car comes to a stop, I'm startled from my reverie.

"We're here," Daphne says.

I look around at the nondescript building. I never would've guessed that this was anything war related, but then I realize that's the whole point. You wouldn't want to broadcast where one of the "headquarters" is. That's a recipe for a target on your back if I've ever heard one.

"You should probably stay here. They wouldn't want me bringing a stranger inside."

I nod in understanding. I didn't think of that when we left her place, but they are probably extremely careful about who knows about this location.

I lean over, giving her a tender but heated kiss before she unbuckles her seat belt and gets out of the car. I watch her ass sway as she walks away from me, and I can't help but groan. I haven't nearly had my fill of her yet, and I pray to anyone or anything listening that I'll get to have more time with her. We just started our journey with each other. We need more time. *I* need more time.

I'm in the car for about twenty minutes before she reemerges, wondering what we'll find at my wreckage site. Will we be able to find my helicopter? I have a feeling that it's my only way of returning home. Then again, I have no idea how it happened in the first place, so I could be completely wrong.

Daphne returns to the car, looking more relieved than when she went in. That has to be good, right?

"They're going to send a team out to try and rescue the hostages. I told them everything I know."

That same relief spills through me, and I feel my shoulders drop marginally. I didn't realize how much that was weighing on me.

"I was also informed that I'll be working in the same camp. We've reclaimed it, which means we should be able to go see your helicopter."

My breath whooshes out of me. I feel like I've been punched in the gut.

"All right, let's see what we can find then."

Chapter 26

Daphne

I pull up close to the healer's tent, but far enough away that no one can spot us. I don't want people to think that I'm coming in today, or to see people in need and feel obligated to hop in. This isn't about that right now.

Noah and I get out of the car and he looks around.

"Does any of this look familiar?" I ask.

He squints around, nodding slightly. "I think so. I think my chopper is over that way." He points in the direction opposite the tent.

I grab his hand and we start walking. My heart rate increases with every step we take. I can't describe it, but I feel like this is about to change things irrevocably.

Storm clouds are gathering in the distance, but they're too far away to affect us. It doesn't take long to reach the area where he went down. Unfortunately, the entire site is a wreck.

Debris everywhere. We walk through it, making sure not to miss anything, but it's not easy. I see the results of war on a regular basis, but not like this.

The battle has moved on from this area, but they haven't cleaned up here yet. Luckily, there aren't any dead bodies, but I can smell the stench of it. Multiple planes were shot down, and bullets litter the battlefield. I look over at Noah to see his eyes looking slightly misty, his jaw clenched, and face red.

"What is it?" I ask.

"I never thought I would witness something like this. At least not anytime soon. I didn't join the military for a reason. I've never wanted to see war, especially not up close and personal like this. Not to mention that this may be the most noble cause to fight for in history. It's just hard to see in person. I've of course learned about it, and seen videos and pictures, but this is so much different." His voice is hoarse, and it cracks at the end, a single tear slipping free.

I grab his hand, squeezing. "I know it's hard. I'm still not used to it, even after all this time. It never gets any easier. But like you said, it is for the most noble cause I can think of."

We continue on our way, there being nothing else to say on the subject. It's unavoidable. At least here.

After another fifteen minutes, he finally spots it. He points, and I gasp upon seeing it. I knew he was telling the truth, but actually *seeing* it is different.

It's like *nothing* I've ever seen. Even wrecked and half in the ground, it looks so technologically advanced. I know Noah said that helicopters were invented around this time, and I've seen the sketch of da Vinci's helicopter, but this is just… There are no words.

I stand there with my mouth hanging open. He looks back

and chuckles at me. "Did you not believe me?"

"You know I did, but having it here in front of me is something else entirely."

"Want to see the inside?"

My eyes are big, and my heart pounds even harder in my chest, but I nod and follow him.

"The nose of the chopper is what's in the ground, along with the blades, but we should still be able to open the doors."

He walks up to it, and with a little finagling, gets the door on the right side open. It's a little awkward getting in with it tilting forward, but Noah helps me.

I'm unable to sit in it, but I lean against the seat with my hip. Noah makes his way around the outside, and in the next moment, he's inside with me.

He shows me all of the knobs and buttons, and I press some of them, pretending that I can actually fly this thing.

"So, what are we looking for?" I ask.

"I'm not sure. Anything unusual. I don't see anything strange though. Everything belongs here," he says as rain starts to fall. I guess the storm finally made its way to us.

I'm about to respond when the ground starts shaking underneath us. I grip the seat hard. I'm already in here precariously, and this is making me incredibly unsteady. Just when I start to shout at Noah that we should get out, lightning strikes in front of us, bright, disorienting, and ear-splitting. I cry out in alarm, moving one of my hands to cover my ear.

Before we can do anything, another strike hits. This time it's not in front of us though. It hits *us*.

Everything goes dark as I'm temporarily blinded, and when my sight finally returns, everything I know is gone.

Chapter 27

Noah

When the world stops shaking and goes quiet, I open my eyes. I'm home. My breath escapes me in a whoosh. At least this time there are no angry Germans shooting me out of the sky.

I instinctively look next to me. I breathe another sigh of relief when I see that Daphne is with me, and unharmed. She looks around, disoriented. I want to tell her it's nothing compared to how I entered the 1940s, but refrain. She appears shaken enough.

"Are you okay?" I ask her, my eyes roaming every part of her I can see. She looks physically fine.

She nods slowly. "I think so. What was that?"

"We just time traveled. And we still have no idea how. There must be some connection between this helicopter and lightning. Honestly, I'm surprised it happened this time since we weren't moving or in the air, but apparently that isn't necessary."

She nods her head again, in a daze.

"Fuck. Daphne, I don't know if I'll be able to get you back home."

Her gaze snaps to mine at that. Tears fill her eyes, and I swear again, but she stops me before I can say more.

"I'm not sure I want to go back," she admits quietly.

I freeze, not moving in case I scare her off. I'm not sure this is real.

She sees the expression on my face. "I'm tired, Noah. I'm so tired. I don't know if I can take *years* of this war." Her voice breaks at the end, and I grip her arm across the helicopter, even though it's awkward.

When she starts crying in earnest, I curse and get out of the helicopter, moving over to her side and opening the door. I have her out and cradled in my arms within seconds. I sink us down onto the ground, pulling her into my lap. I stroke her back soothingly, and when she pulls back to look at me I search her eyes.

"What about your family?"

Her brow furrows. "Is there some way we can find out what happened to them?"

"Actually, we should be able to. It might take us a while though. In the meantime, let's get home."

"Okay," she says, finally taking in our surroundings. "Where are we?"

"Astoria, Oregon. I'll need to figure out how to get us back to Portland."

Fuck. I have no idea how I'm going to explain the helicopter or my absence. I wonder if I could just tell them the truth. They had to have noticed my disappearance, right? I mean, I vanished out of the fucking *sky.* I'll worry about that later though.

For now, I search the chopper. I had my phone and wallet with me on my original flight, and after some searching, I find both. My wallet is on the floor of the passenger side, and my phone, while dead and cracked, is between the center console and my seat. I sigh in relief. Maybe we will just stay in a hotel tonight. I don't think I have the energy to make the trip back to Portland right now, and Daphne looks like she needs a good meal and a nap.

I look around. Fuck. We're going to have to go to the airport. Maybe one of the guys there can take us to the hotel down the road, as it's too far to walk.

We're exactly where my helicopter went missing, except it's currently on the ground instead of in the air. I take a deep breath and lead her to the airport. Nothing for it now.

We reach it fairly quickly, and I squeeze her hand before we head inside. Dennis looks up in confusion. He didn't see anyone land. His brows shoot up in surprise when he spots me.

"Noah! What are you doing here? We've been looking for you. We were so concerned after you went missing the other day."

Dennis owns the airport here. He's the one I need to talk to about this. Fuck. I can't lie to him. The helicopter is *wrecked.* Not to mention riddled with bullets. Here goes nothing.

"Well, funny story. I was somehow transported back in time."

He starts laughing.

"I'm serious, Dennis."

He scoffs.

"You *know* my chopper vanished out of thin air. How can you explain that? I traveled back to World War II in France, and was shot down. The helicopter is outside. Go look if you don't believe me."

Disbelief colors his features.

"Dennis. *Go look.*"

He doesn't say anything, but gets up from his seat and walks out the door. At least he's listening to me about that. Daphne and I wait in tense silence until he comes back.

His face is ashen when he returns. His eyes meet mine as he opens his mouth to speak, but no words come out.

"It's true, Dennis. This is Daphne. She's from England and the time I traveled to. She traveled back with me."

"It's very nice to meet you," she says quietly. I almost laugh at the absurdity of her manners at a time like this. Weirdly enough, that seems to do the trick.

His eyes nearly bug out of his head, and I know what he's experiencing. It's not only evident that she's from England, but there's something about her speech that is different from how we speak in these times.

"You're telling the truth?" he whispers, and I'm so shocked that he believes me that all I can do is nod.

Chapter 28

Daphne

I can't believe that this man is taking Noah at his word. I mean, of course it's true, and these events, not to mention the state of the helicopter and my presence, are hard to explain, but humans are not well-known for trusting extraordinary things, even if the evidence of it is right in front of their eyes.

The two men talk for a while, but I'm so exhausted that I don't register what they say. I feel dead on my feet, and I don't know how Noah is still functioning. I collapse into a chair in the lobby while they chat, and after fifteen minutes or so, their words finally break through.

"Dennis, would you mind giving us a ride? We need to stay in a hotel for the night, and my girl here needs some food and a bed."

Dennis nods. "Of course, man. Let me tell the others that I'm leaving."

Noah returns to me and helps me stand. "We can relax soon, baby girl. It won't take us long to get to the hotel, and then after a nap, I'll take you to dinner. How does that sound?"

I almost moan. "Like heaven."

He chuckles but takes my hand in his, leading me outside. Dennis joins us shortly after, leading us to his car. His *car*. It looks absolutely *nothing* like the vehicles I'm used to. I hesitantly get in, looking around curiously. I don't know if I'll ever get used to this. Granted, I just got here, but I have a feeling this will always be a novelty. I was raised in a time that was so far behind this, so going from one to the other is jarring.

I take in the city as we drive, and am shocked to see how much busier it is. There are so many more people here, but they seem happy and at peace. I breathe a sigh of relief. I didn't realize how used to being in a time of war I was.

We pull up to a gorgeous hotel that is literally *on* the river. I look at the sign to see the Cannery Pier Hotel.

"This is my favorite place to stay when I'm here," Noah says.

I admire it with new eyes. I like it even more now.

We exit the vehicle, and Dennis shakes Noah's hand. "I'll pick you back up tomorrow, yeah?"

Noah nods. "That would be great, Dennis. Thank you so much."

"You're welcome. It was a pleasure to meet you, Daphne."

"Thank you. You as well, Dennis."

"Oh wait, before you leave, I brought this. I figured you'd need one."

Dennis hands Noah a cord with a plug on the end.

"Oh thanks, man. My phone died, and I don't have a charger. Hopefully it'll turn on for me. I don't know how fucked up it got in the crash."

"Well, if I don't hear from you I'll just come by at eleven."

He nods and we head into the hotel, and I gasp in amazement. After, of course, jumping a foot in the air when the doors slide open automatically. I try not to look obviously out of place, but it's extremely difficult. Everywhere I look there are things that I want to study, and that I can't wrap my head around.

Noah checks us in, and the receptionist looks at us strangely, but doesn't say anything. I suppose it seems odd that we don't have any luggage, not to mention our clothing.

Noah grabs my hand and leads me over to the elevator. I marvel at how smooth and fast it is. When we arrive at our room, he swipes a little card over a panel under the handle. It beeps and turns green before he opens the door.

"How did you do that? Was it unlocked?"

He chuckles. "No. This is our key," he says, holding up the plastic.

"Excuse me, what? That is not a key."

"Hotels use these as keys now. We don't use them for our houses and things, although we have a lot of different ways to lock something without it being an actual key."

I have a hard time wrapping my mind around this, but I simply nod and follow him inside. The room is incredible. I gasp upon seeing the view out the window. We're literally over the water. I go over to the balcony and open the door to stand outside. Noah comes up behind me and wraps his arms around me, his front pressing to my back as a massive boat heads up the river.

"What river is this?"

"The Columbia."

We stand there, just enjoying each other and the chilly fall air. I yawn dramatically, and Noah's chuckle vibrates against my back. "Let's get you to bed. You've had a big day. You need to rest."

"You've had a big day too."

"Yes, but I've done this before. I know how disorienting it is. Especially having it not be your own time. It's been less exhausting and jarring for me coming home."

He's right. That's exactly how I feel. Not only exhausted, but my entire life has essentially been uprooted. Everything around me is unfamiliar. Except him.

We head inside, and I collapse onto the massive bed.

Chapter 29

Noah

We take a nap, both exhausted after the events of the day. Well, week really. It's dark when I wake, but I sigh in relief when I see that it's still early enough to get dinner. I look over at Daphne, frowning at her clothes. We need to find something more time appropriate to wear.

I quietly get up, letting her rest for a little bit longer. I grab the hotel key and sneak out, wanting to see if they have anything in the gift shop. The receptionist gives me a funny look again as I come down, but I ignore her. I find us two shirts with the Cannery Pier Hotel embossed on them. Eh. Not my first pick, but we really don't have any other options.

I also grab us a bottle of wine and bring everything back upstairs. Daphne stirs as the door opens, and I'm glad she didn't wake up alone while I was downstairs. I see the confusion on her face as consciousness sets in, but then realization when all the memories flood back.

"Hungry?" I ask. She must be starving. I know I am.

She nods.

"Let's go out to dinner. I grabbed us each a shirt to change into." I hand her said shirt, and she smiles gratefully at me before stripping off her own.

My eyes roam her chest, and I almost stop her from putting her new one on, but just then her stomach rumbles loudly. Fuck. Food first. Then dessert.

She must see the desire in my eyes when she finishes dressing because a lovely blush rises to her cheeks. Before I end up going against my plans and ravish her, I turn and unplug my phone. I'm grateful to my past self for remembering to plug it in before we collapsed into bed. I'm even more grateful when it turns on for me.

I pocket it and change into my own shirt. It's ugly and we look like dipshit tourists, but oh well. Nothing we can do about it until I get us home.

I turn and grab Daphne's hand, pulling her up and hanging on to her as we leave the room. Unfortunately, this hotel doesn't have kitchens, but there is a restaurant right down the street that has amazing food.

We take a seat by the windows that overlook the water and order drinks, Daphne a red wine, and me a wheat beer. I also get us some bruschetta while we decide what to eat.

When the server brings our drinks and appetizer, I order the fish and chips and she orders the alfredo. As soon as he's gone we dig into our food with gusto. The bruschetta is gone way too quickly, but between how hungry we are and the quality of the food, it really didn't stand a chance.

Daphne takes everything in with wide eyes, and I know how

strange this must be for her. At least I had the advantage of knowing the history when I traveled. She doesn't have the same luxury. Everything is new for her instead of old. I take her hand across the table and grip it tightly.

"It gets easier. You'll adapt quickly."

Her curious and overwhelmed gaze meets mine. She looks like she doesn't quite believe me, but she nods all the same. Our food comes then, and we are once again consumed with our meal.

The server clears our plates and I pay the tab. When we get back to the hotel room, I turn on the light in the luxurious bathroom.

"Bath or shower?"

She eyes both, looking longingly at the tub. I'm positive she's going to choose that option, but when I head over to turn it on, she speaks up.

"Shower. I want to wash my hair and body, and that's not as easy in the tub," she states, even though she's giving the shower a dubious look.

I don't blame her. There are so many nozzles and buttons on the shower that even I had a hard time with it when I first started staying here. I nod, squeezing past her to turn everything on. I step out while she undresses and pour us each a glass of wine.

When I come back into the bathroom, she's in the shower, the steam billowing around her naked body, and I let out a pained groan. She's so sexy, and I feel like she doesn't even realize it.

She turns to see me staring at her from the doorway and gives me a knowing smile. "Will you wash my back?"

I need no further invitation. I undress and join her.

Chapter 30

Daphne

Noah opens the shower door and hands me my wine. I take a grateful drink before setting it on the ledge. I already have shampoo in my hair, which smells delightfully of mint. The shower stall is small, so we have to squeeze together for us both to fit, which is fine by me.

"Rinse your hair. I'll start washing your body," Noah tells me.

His heated gaze indicates that he'd rather get me dirty instead of clean, but I follow his instructions. For now. But only because I'm dying to wash this day off of me.

I tip my head back, the suds flowing down my back. The heated water mixed with the exquisite pressure of the shower-head makes me never want to leave. That feeling is even more heightened when Noah's soapy hands skate over every inch of my skin.

I apply conditioner to my hair, and he scrubs down my back.

There are definite perks to showering with another person.

"My turn," I tell him, switching spots with him. He got to explore my body. Now I want to do the same to him.

He gives me a devilish smile, but obliges, passing me the body wash. I apply a liberal amount to my hands before reaching out and running circles over his toned chest. He quickly washes his hair, but doesn't close his eyes. In fact, they haven't left me since I started touching him.

After rinsing everything off himself, I switch spots with him again. I need to get the conditioner out of my hair. I tilt my head back and close my eyes, but they pop back open a moment later when I feel Noah's mouth running along the wet seam of my pussy. I gasp and moan, shoving my hands into his hair. I look down, admiring how captivating he is on his knees in front of me.

He stares back up at me. "Finish rinsing your hair, baby girl. I'm going to make you come and then we're going to go back to bed where I can fuck you properly."

His words alone make my orgasm start to build. I don't think I've ever rinsed my hair more quickly or half-heartedly. When I'm finished, I grip on to his head as his arms wrap around my waist to support me. I fuck his face with abandon, thrusting my hips against his mouth and reveling in the things he can do with it.

"Noah," I moan out, almost incoherently. "I need…I need…" I don't know what I need. More. Less. Everything.

He seems to understand though, and he doubles his efforts. I reach up and toy with my own breasts, making him growl in approval. The vibration pushes me even higher, and just before I tip off the edge, a finger pushes into my tight back hole. The feeling is so foreign that it almost keeps me from my climax, but when Noah nips down on my clit and slides his finger in farther, I'm a goner.

I cry out, going rigid in his arms, my body spasming around his digit. He continues working me until I completely relax in his hold. My legs have given out and I know I would be a crumpled mess on the floor if not for his arms supporting me.

He stands, giving me a detonating kiss. I taste myself on his lips, and I moan against him.

"I need you. Daphne, I need you."

He shuts off the water, and I snag a towel to quickly wrap my hair in before he basically shoves me on the bed in his haste to have me.

There's no buildup, no slow escalation. As soon as I'm on the bed, he's over me and pushing into me. I clench around him, my body still buzzing from the orgasm he gave me in the shower.

"Fuckkkk. God, baby girl. You're so tight and wet. Perfect."

He claims me. There's no other word for it. It's frenzied, wild, and utter *bliss.* I hold on to his back for dear life as his tongue plunders my mouth in search of my own. My legs wrap around him, bringing him even deeper into my heat. I swear with every thrust I can feel the tip of his length kissing my womb, and his pelvis brushing against my sensitive clit.

"I can't last, Daphne. I need you to come for me again. Milk me. Make me spill inside you."

God, he has the dirtiest mouth. I fucking love it.

"Come. Now," he orders, and my body can't help but obey.

I'm thrown headfirst into my climax. I scream his name, and I'm sure even people on the other side of the Columbia can hear it.

"Hell yes, baby girl. I told you I would have you screaming

for me. I'm coming. Fuck."

He pumps into me once, twice, three times before he stills, his hot length twitching inside of me. Then, he collapses on top of me, and we lie there, holding each other until our heart beats calm and we're drifting off to sleep.

Chapter 31

Noah

The next morning, we wake late, utterly spent after the week we've had. Even though this hotel doesn't have a restaurant, they do serve a continental breakfast. It's nothing special, but it does the trick at filling our bellies. Not to mention that after we were stuck in the warehouse, this feels like a five-star dining experience in comparison.

I text Dennis to let him know that we're ready to be picked up whenever he has the time. Within ten minutes he responds that he's on his way. Daphne and I gather all of our belongings from the room, check out, and are waiting out front for him by the time he arrives. He brings us back to the airport, not saying much, but I can tell that he believes us even more than he did yesterday. There are bags under his eyes, and I'm willing to bet he didn't sleep and spent all his time since I last saw him doing research and inspecting the chopper.

When we get there, he looks at me hesitantly. "Are you going to be okay flying back on your own?"

His question makes me finally realize our situation. I'm going to have to get back in a helicopter and fly myself and Daphne back to Portland. Can I do that after everything that happened? The last time I flew, I was shot down. Not to mention that the last two times I was in a helicopter, I time traveled. I'm sure I've got some PTSD from that, but I realize that while I'm nervous and more than a little apprehensive, I know I'll be able to fly as well as I normally do. And I know myself. The best way to get over this and to move forward will be to just get back on the horse. And seeing as we obviously won't be in the same helicopter, I think we'll be fine on the time traveling aspect too.

"Yes. It'll be a little nerve-racking, but I'll be fine. After all, I've had a few close calls in the past. The only way forward is through. And it's not a long flight."

He studies me for a long moment before nodding. "All right then. Text me when you land. And I didn't tell you yesterday, but I'm so relieved you're okay."

He claps me on the shoulder and brings me in for a typical male embrace. I return the pat on his back before breaking away and heading toward the waiting helicopter. Nerves build in my stomach as I open the passenger door for Daphne, but I push past them. I want to keep flying, and this is the first step. I help her inside and when she's seated, I strap her in, thoroughly checking everything. Twice. When I'm sure everything is safe and looks as it should, I look over at Daphne.

"Ready?"

She has a nervous expression on her face, but there's excitement there too. She nods, and we take off, leaving Astoria behind us. Daphne lets out a squeal, and it makes me smile. I'm glad I get to share this with her.

It takes us roughly an hour to fly to Portland, and I'm relieved that within the first few minutes, the anxiety I had about flying seems to melt away. I still love flying. This has been my happy place ever since my first flight. Whenever I can, I peek over at Daphne. She has a huge smile on her face, wonder painting every line of her features as she takes in the sights of the city before us.

"Welcome to Portland," I tell her.

She smiles at me, and for the first time since we traveled back to my time, she seems happy.

We land with no issues, and the guys at the airport give me shit about our shirts, but underneath I can see the relief that I'm alive and well. I have no idea what Dennis told them, but I'm grateful that none of them ask me any questions.

My car is exactly where I left it, and I let out a little sigh of relief as I sit in the driver's seat. It feels good to get back to normal with my girl at my side.

"We should stop and get you some clothes and things."

"That would be nice."

Luckily, there's a Target right down the street from my house, and we make quick work of getting her multiple sets of clothes (even though she's appalled at the choices, and almost scandalized by what she sees), grooming products, and some food. I was running low when I left.

When we're finished, I take us home. It's nothing special, but I've always cherished it. This was where I struck out on my own for the first time. I knew nobody when I moved here. This place became my sanctuary.

Daphne takes in my space, and I feel slightly vulnerable. "It's lovely," she finally tells me, making something in my chest loosen.

I start a load of laundry, figuring she'll want to wash her new clothes. For now, I get her one of my shirts and a pair of sweats. She's swimming in them, but I can't deny how much I like seeing her in my clothes. I change as well, and then I make us a quick lunch of sandwiches. When we're done eating, I break out my laptop.

"Okay, let's see what we can find."

It takes some digging, but after a few hours, I'm able to finally find something concrete for her.

Her mom died in the '70s. I can't figure out the cause of death, but it looks like she lived a nice long life. Her brother had a child, but he died in the '50s from cancer. I'm also able to find a record of Daphne. It states that she went missing in the war, and after no one was able to find her, she was declared dead.

When I look back at her, she has tears in her eyes, but a smile on her face. "None of them died in the war."

"Is that what you wanted to know?"

She nods, tears streaming down her cheeks in earnest now.

"What do you want to do, Daphne?"

She takes a deep breath before giving me a sweet kiss. My heart is in my throat as I wait for her to answer.

"I want to stay here with you."

"You do?"

"Yes, Noah. I want a life away from war and poverty. I want a life with *you*."

I crush her to my chest, kissing her with everything I have in me. She's *mine*. And she's not going anywhere.

Chapter 32

Daphne—Three months later…

The last few months have been surreal. Not only am I adjusting to being in a new relationship and living with Noah, I've also had to navigate this new time I was thrust into. It's actually been more difficult than I thought it would. Technology is something that I have no inclination for, but am slowly learning how to handle.

Noah asked me what I wanted to do after things settled down a bit, and at first I wasn't sure if I wanted to go back into nursing or not. The war was so difficult, and it made me reluctant to get back into the field. But eventually, I realized that this is a part of myself that I love and have a passion for. I know it won't be a walk in the park, but it will be less stressful and scarring than my previous situation.

That being said, I don't know any of the new procedures or technologies that go along with today's field of medicine. Soooo,

I'm back in school. It's actually been incredibly interesting. I'm impressed, and if I'm being honest, a little intimidated by the strides that have been made since my time.

Noah, on the other hand, is almost done with his helicopter training, and he's incredibly excited. At first, I was reluctant and anxious to have him get back in the aircrafts, nervous that he would somehow end up time traveling again, but everything has been fine. As far as we can tell, the incidents were tied to the specific helicopter. Dennis had the whole thing examined, and they were able to find a few things that were out of place, including a crossed wire and a blown fuse, but since it was shot down out of the sky and crash-landed, there's no way to know if any of that was present before and caused the traveling.

The school has offered him a position after he finishes his check ride and he's thrilled. He really didn't want to look for jobs all over the States and potentially uproot us. He loves this part of the country, and I do too. It's grown on me, and even though I miss my home and my family, and occasionally my own time period, I wouldn't go back. I love the life we've built together.

One thing I have done is researched my family line. I know my brother ended up having a child, and I want to see if I can reach out to her in some way. She's still alive and has her own family, but they're in England. As much as I want to contact her, I'm unsure of how to go about it. It's not like I can just email her and say, "Oh hi, I'm your long lost aunt that time traveled and is somehow younger than you. Want to meet?"

I bring it up to Noah one day. "What do you think I should do?"

"Well, obviously you can't tell her the truth yet, but you could say that you're a distant relative and you discovered her while doing research on your ancestry. She might not be willing to have contact with you, some people don't, but you can at least try."

This man. "God, you're brilliant," I say, kissing him firmly on the lips.

He preens at the compliment. "Not as brilliant as you, baby doll."

I chuckle. "So, what do you have in mind for tonight?"

"I was thinking I could make you a lovely dinner, and we could eat out on the porch by the fire and listen to Nat King Cole, and then I'll take you to bed and make love to you until you can no longer stay awake. How does that sound?"

My knees go a little weak, but I manage a raspy "That sounds nice."

He gives me a knowing chuckle. "What do you want for dinner?"

"On second thought, how about we have dessert first?" My voice is husky with desire, but I don't care.

"Whatever the lady wants," he whispers as he closes in on my mouth. He gives me a heated kiss before sweeping me up in his arms and carrying me into our bedroom.

As he lays me out on the bed, all I can think about is how much I love this man. I can't believe that fate saw fit to literally have him crash into my life, but I'm grateful every day to whatever impossible scenario brought us together.

The End.

About the Author

L.J. Burkhart is a fantasy and romance author, as she loves all things paranormal and passionate. She has been a lifelong writer, starting with songs and poetry in the third grade, before eventually moving on to novels in her early twenties. When she isn't coming up with dramatic plot twists and steamy sex scenes, you can find her doing yoga, hanging out with her best bitches, baking, or reading, curled up on the couch with her husband and dog with a big glass of red wine.

You can connect with me on:
🌐 https://www.ljburkhart.com

Subscribe to my newsletter:

✉ http://eepurl.com/hRZzz5